The Naked Pharaoh

Henry Mpagazi

Published by Volo Press, LLC (VoloPressBooks.com).
Cover and interior illustrations by
Henry Amin Mpagazi and Jabari Amin Mpagazi.

Cover formatting by Volo Press Books, LLC.
Copy editing by Emily Ham.
Copyright 07-25-2011
TXU 1-765-509

The Naked Pharaoh

ISBN: 978-0692146446
10 9 8 7 6 5 4 3 2 1
1. History 2. History – Africa – Egypt
First Edition
Printed and bound in the United States of America.
First printing July 2019.

ACKNOWLEDGEMENT

Catherine Spearmon,

Mother of Fleeta Najeebah and Jabari, and for her tenacity to maintain during my absence; truly one of God's babysitters.

 Henry,

   "I always remember those silk stockings you bought me 50 years ago." For your labor of love, and unending dedication to searching out the truth of our history, and sharing your understanding in words and art for enrichment of our lives for many generations to come. I feel honored to know you.

Love,

Vera

In Memory of
Mark Clark
Rahn 'Ducho' Dennis

Illustrations

All illustrations created by the authors.

Preface

Scholars say prose without imagination lacks passion. This advice has been put into practice, here. The conversations shared in this manuscript are imaginary, recalled from dreams, yet somehow vivid memories, unexplained. I've learned that the ancient Nuba, indigenous of South Sudan, used a hand-rubbing process to decorate the walls of their huts. The finished work produced walls colored with blue sheen, caused by graphite in the dirt. Millennia later, that same blue coloring was found on the walls inside tombs of *Amarna* Pharaohs in *"The Lower Valley of River Nile."* The knowledge and my pencil drawing entitled: *"The Naked Pharaoh"* caused me to believe a story was waiting somewhere, so here 'tis.

History confirms people from southern Sudan settled the Nile Valley. For the most part, how they traveled and the problems faced remain a mystery. So, my imagination wandered into southern Sudan, created a gathering of Nuba, and trekked them North into the lower valley of the River Nile.

The beginning chapter is a brief narrative of Egypt with mention of events that caused its ancient decline. The second chapter imagines south Sudan a millennia ago and starts off by following the travails of a mannish child named Erastus.

Henry Mpagazi

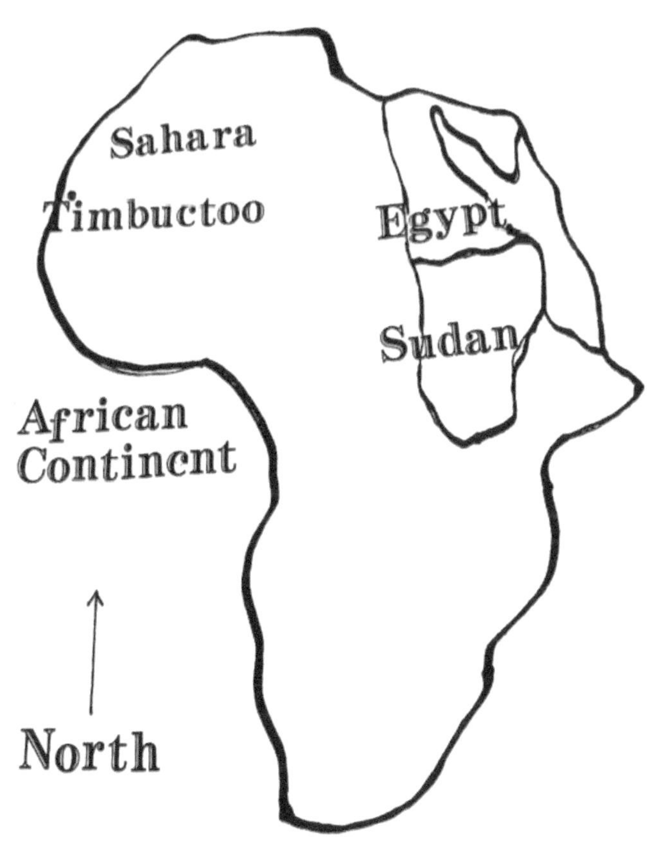

Sahara
Timbuctoo
Egypt
Sudan
African
Continent
North

CHAPTER # 1
ON TIME AND AT PLACE

"Who nursed the doubtful child of civilization on the wandering banks of the life-giving River Nile? And gave to the teeming nations of the earth (by way of Greece) disciplines of philosophy?" An age-old question asked by Michael DeAnang, poet laureate from West Africa.

Bilued el-Sudan means "*The Land of Blacks*." It is located northeast on the African continent; and from its southern hills indigenous *Nuba* went north into ancient Egypt. As time passed, the fertile valley of the River Nile branded Nuba, "*Amarna.*" And the Nuba, responsible for leaving proof of stay, there; *did not stir!* Excavations of *Tell el-Amarna the* ancient metropolis reveal Nuba stride into civilization was carefully pondered, as evidenced by historian Barbara Watterson's work "Ancient Egypt Age of Revolution." Pictured on page #83 is furniture which favors thoughtfulness: an ageless toilet stool!

The lower valley of the River Nile is a gigantic oasis, and the thriving growth exists mostly due to the River Nile, a north flowing pillager of nutrients from Lake Victoria, the second largest freshwater body on earth. Residing in Sub-Sahara's Uganda, we may try to imagine when Lake Victoria originally overflowed, causing water to cascade north. However, to precisely date such an occurrence would be akin to dating the first drop of rain that ever hit dirt, so suffice to say, there comes a time while scribbling when only a period can halt one's imagination.

Millennia passed; the Nile carved its way north to the Mediterranean Sea, forcing life on a valley which in turn grew with abundance. When the Nuba arrived, they couldn't avoid stubbing toes against watermelons that lay about. According to Percy Newberry's "The Ancient Botany," the Nile valley was replete with foods which included an abundance of grains, nuts, flowers, spices, and of course watermelon. With all those different tastes, the makings of soul food certainly had to find their beginnings in there, somewhere.

Having the knowledge of seeds and an unlimited source of water, well-fed Nuba had time for unhurried ponder; and that prepared them for many endeavors. The *Pyramids of Giza,* as well as many other colossi which remain over modern-day Egypt, speaks of the Nuba's incalculable toils. While modern Egyptians may delight in treasures which still stand, there are those which are preserved against bygone plunderers. The granite bust of Ramesses the Second as well as his *Speos* at Abu Simbel, remain somewhere; and the *Sphinx of Chephren* still stands guard as it did centuries ago when all roads in the known world led there.

Ancient Egypt was a region which cultivated civility while other nations brawled, but the emerging civilization welcomed all: those of good will, as well as those who were contentious. Thus, the knowledge Amarna developed over millennia was coveted, needed, and often time usurped.

Many great thinkers of ancient Greece (Plato, Socrates and others) were simply history's most infamous plagiarists. The discipline requirements of learned philosophy could not have originated in warring Greece for two important reasons. First, the Grecian government disallowed the teaching of African Culture. Secondly, how can one think virtuously when continually defending oneself? These and other findings are well documented in Professor George G.M. James' work "Stolen Legacy." Consequently, the philosophy behind the thought *"Man, Know Thyself"* was many centuries old before Greece finally recognized its worth.

In 332 B.C. Alexander the Great, imperial conqueror from Macedonia, began his conquest; marching south through Halicarnassus then turning east into Cilician Gates following Mediterranean's eastern shore south into Ancient Egypt. Along the way, cities Issus, Byblos, and Tyre, (Persian Empire annexes at that time) became spoils of war for the marauding conqueror.

Alexander the Great was 24 years old when he entered Egypt, and what he saw must have been stunning. He was in the midst of a civilization alien to his way of thinking. The towering sculptures of stone, which peered over his head, bore images of black folk. We can only imagine Alexander must have been amazed by such an advanced civilization. History confirms that he ordered his army to plunder, defacing statues and committing other vandalism.

Perhaps during a lull in the destruction, an exhausted captain approached his commander.

"Sir," he said, "we have torched the libraries, disfigured noses on all statues we found including that black ass *Sphinx* way over yonder; but I think I need a bigger hammer to crush them Pyramids."

"Very well, Captain," responded Alexander, probably clearing his throat. "I shall allow the Pyramids to stand a few more days"

"Thank you, Sir," replied the captain, as he rushed somewhere to sleep; thinking, "I fear my commander has lost his wine-drinking mind."

A tired captain fell into slumber,
Alexander the Great fell into plunder.

Ancient Egypt was in decline. Alexander the Great, as other invaders before and after, did their part to hasten the cause, usurping science, art, literature, philosophy and many other disciplines Amarna had developed over centuries. Confiscating literature and attempting to deface monuments that which eventually contributed to prosperity.

Trekking Nuba had steadfast cleave,
Pare not rind us nurture need.
Severed seed impedes life breed,
Indeed, indeed, take heed.

CHAPTER #2
UNCLE REMOS

Join us on our tale and journey with the Nuba as they emerge from the fog of antiquity. Imagine mud squishing between toes as they trampled about hunting and gathering food. The abundance of food in certain seasons and scarcity at other times helped Nuba understand the purpose of seed.

Sowing and reaping, replaced hunting and gathering; and the once nomadic Nuba settled, constructing villages all over southern Sudan. In a world of lingering hunger, the knowledge of seed arrived not a moment too soon. Although passing of time erased Nuba first sow to harvest; logic now tattles Nuba patience and perseverance ensured the will of *God*, done.

The journey from the muddy fields of Sudan to atop Pyramids of Giza proved to be long, arduous, and even at times uncanny. But it is the reason modern-day Egypt is monumental to the creation of civilization.

To proximate oneself in the presence of Pharaoh Tutankhamen's unearthed treasures, exposes the absurdity of Napoleon Bonaparte's assertion that "history is fables we agree on." Napoleon's narcissism of thought allowed scholars to be exposed to falsification of recorded history, and denies them a factual basis for study.

Now the presence of mind for civilization had to start somewhere, so destruction of ancient Egypt's centuries-old libraries ensured historical facts on the matter would be questionable, to say the least. And according to anthropologists, Sub-Saharans was responsible for laying many foundations during the process of evolution. So we imagine (for the sake of these conversations) the first conscious thought for civilization came from an ancient village in southern Sudan where a certain man-child was born.

Imagine hills that surrounded the village echoing his first cry. The boy must have had loud lungs from the womb, but when the name *Erastus* was whispered into his ear, it is told that he stopped crying. Erastus was born from linage of proven leaders and it showed when he continued walking after his first step. In later years, when children his age gathered to play, he stood alone with arms folded and head erect, bearing the watchful eyes of a sentinel. The Nuba's favorite son had made his presence. He grew tall, strapping, and carried himself on feet big enough to balance a totem pole, strolling about the village a vision of long awaited native son.

Born the second of three sons from a highly respected monarchal family, Erastus' coming was foretold. His older brother, who had the family birthright, showed very little interest in leadership and spent most of his time hunting. The third son was extremely eccentric and did nothing more than mimic women.

The village youth made fun of the confused third brother until the village *Mak* (chief) proclaimed,

"Leave him be. If you are living, you belong," said he, and so it was.

Erastus' lust for power surfaced early, and he wasted little time positioning himself for leadership. His boldness showed during the three day "Rite of Passage" ceremony, the body piercing ritual that tests one's tolerance to pain. Erastus *did not stir!*

After rite of passage man children of the Nuba are considered grown, thus Erastus' adulthood status quickly added urgency to his ambitions. However, when told a rise to Village Mak was fraught with obstacles, Erastus wondered why he shouldn't forgo the village-level leadership and seek the ultimate position: Mak of Nuba. In the state of Mississippi when a problem become more challenging we allude "The Mississippi mud just thickened." So it was for Erastus, he must now face a fifteen-member governing congress led by Uncle Remus, the oldest man ever seen.

During Uncle Remus' leadership, the Nuba expanded considerably; now feeble, the wise elder possessed less strength to govern effectively. Time exacted its toll on the governing *Methuselah* and the Nuba's need for a younger Mak was evident. Erastus considered himself the chosen one and shall rely on "your time has come" certainty to aid his ambitions.

Early one morning, Erastus departed the village with a water gourd at his side and a message for the Nuba in mind. His plan was to travel about the nation and discuss concepts and ideas with the hope that being well acquainted would ensure a position of strength. However, his first village stop brought into focus an unforeseen snag. The village Mak's daughter had taken up with a man, and there was no *guba* dusk (peanuts) for the ceremony. The villagers were in no mood for discussion until the Mak was satisfied. "Go find some *guba* dusk," they told Erastus.

Erastus went back home and bartered for a pouch of *guba* dusk. When he returned, the villagers invited him to eat and talk, and that day he made many friends. When Erastus finally departed, he had a water gourd and a pouch of *guba* dusk slung to his side.

As he roamed, Erastus learned that being a good listener was not only rewarding but vital to leadership, a lesson re-enforced often during his travel. One day, half-way between villages, he encountered an elderly, heavy-set woman bartering slices of watermelons.

Surrounded by heaps of the green, oblong fruit, Erastus asked why she offered only slices.

The woman stared at him keenly and said, "One Nuba, one slice."

Erastus took his piece, retreated to the opposite side of the path, and sat on a rock to eat. When he finished, he approached the woman again.

"My name is Erastus," he said, "and one day soon I shall become Mak of Nuba. At the moment I need nourishing to continue my quest."

"That may be so," replied the woman, "but Nuba Mak is one and there are many more Nuba than watermelons. So one Nuba, one slice," she repeated.

It took Erastus a moment to grasp "Watermelon Woman's" message, but he walked away with this wise caution: Unchecked greediness will hinder a nation's survival.

Erastus then turned his attention toward Korongo, a large area inhabited by Nuba of a different tongue. Korongo Nuba were more aggressive than the *Meskin* Erastus kind and did not welcome prying intruders.

Erastus started his walk up a long, inclined path toward a large Korongo village. Halfway up the winding slope, a quartet of men, each armed with spear, emerged from the lush grass and followed him at a distance. Erastus walked onward, but as he neared the village entrance a spear flew over his head and landed directly on the ground in front of him, causing him to stop.

"*Miskin*," said one of the four now standing at his side, "What brings you to Korongo?"

"Remove your spear from my path. The future Mak of Nuba does not answer questions when threatened," Erastus answered.

"Remove it yourself; you're closer than I am," taunted the speaker.

Erastus *did not stir!* He was well aware that touching the spear was taboo. Instead he spoke confidently, "Your leader misunderstood my intentions," pointing towards the one without a spear. "Remove the weapon, and take me to the Village Mak."

"Do as he ordered," replied the leader. "Perhaps the *Miskin* can offer a bit of entertainment before day is done."

The Guards escorted Erastus into the village center, as women folk brought food and water.

After Erastus finished eating, the village Mak appeared and asked Erastus if he was an envoy from Nuba congress.

"No, Honored One. My journey is a personal quest to present myself and become well-known throughout Nuba."

"And for what purpose?" asked the Mak.

"My intent is to become Mak of Nuba. At which time, I plan to advance this nation into a new era."

"You certainly have brassiness. Go ahead, young man, and continue your journey. But keep in mind: We are an aggressive lot. So take this spear with you; it bears my markings. Korongo Nuba will think twice before taking your life."

Erastus bowed as an aide handed him the spear. He gave thanks, then departed.

Eventually Erastus returned home, mindful of all he had learned. Then one night, he secluded himself a short distance from the village to ponder how best to engage the elders. Under the glow of a full moon, Erastus sat on a stump surrounded by clustered trees. Stillness of night engrossed his contemplation.

"I cannot become the Mak of Nuba without the elders' acceptance," he thought. "So my stance must be assertive. Without a show of strength they will reject me as weakness; but if I present myself too boldly, I will be tossed out abruptly for insolence.

"I must exhibit humility in my meeting with the elders," Erastus said aloud, "but not to a fault."

The next morning, Erastus stood at the village center with a large, talking drum. He began a beat recognized by the Nuba as a call to gather. As morning wore on, the booming sounds beckoned the villagers in droves as Erastus' tempo quickened. Erastus was oblivious to the gathering crowd. The drum's complicated rhythms demanded his full attention. Sweat from his brow sparkled like crushed diamonds as the beat went on.

Suddenly! With the ball of his right fist, Erastus struck the drum with a hammer-like stroke and sent a booming sound reverberating through the Nuba hills. He repeated the lick twenty times. After the final stroke, body drenched in sweat, Erastus lifted his arms skyward and proclaimed, "I am Erastus, Mak of Nuba. Let it be told throughout the world!"

Words spoken, Erastus strolled towards the silenced crowd. Many stepped aside, allowing passage, while others bowed. A muscular, little man shouldered the drum and followed Erastus' footsteps. Someone hollered, "Don't drop the drum, Sambo!" However most ominous at the gathering Nuba Elders *did not stir!*

After waiting for time to scatter his bold proclamation and satisfied his words had reached whole of Nuba, Erastus requested a council with the elders, as was his privilege. Although they granted the request, the Nuba elders remained cautious and offered very little welcome to Erastus' pompous and demanding behavior; yet they were equally aware of the Nuba leadership needs. They did not reject the demands outright, but postponed a decision on his proclamation to allow time for thought. The first meeting did not bode well for the potential Mak.

OASIS SIWA
LOWER VALLEY
NILE
ANCIENT EGYPT
RED SEA
Tell el-AMARNA
OASIS FAYUM
THEBES
NILE
SAHARA
NORTH
UPPER VALLEY
NILE
SUDAN
TROPICAL AFRICA
NUBA

The Nuba congress gathered and squabbled for two days. On the third day, a decision was made to send Erastus on an unusual quest, a dare so daunting it would require God's help for success. If Erastus' undertaking satisfied the covenant, then doubts about his self-proclamation would vanish. On the other hand, if Erastus failed during his endeavor, Nuba would have vanquished an irritating "rock" from between their toes. For the elders, either one of those solutions sounded favorable, because unbeknownst to Erastus, they had already spanned the land in search of a younger Mak.

The Elders called a council and sat in a circle, intentionally nudging Erastus to the same spot he declared himself Mak. Erastus made such a commotion with the drum, the whole of the Nuba nation anticipated change. The Nuba congress was a step ahead, however. The proposed dare would take time to complete, therefore slowing any rush to change.

The crowd was bigger that day, teeming with folk anxiously awaiting Erastus' fate. An aide passed the talking stick to the first elder.

"Son of Nuba, if your soul is set, you must go on a journey of our choosing," he said. "Should you return, we shall know you possess strength required of Mak." The talking stick was then passed to the second elder.

"If you accept our dare, listen carefully. We shall build for you a flat-bottom sailing barge that you must sail on dry land north to the lower Nile valley. From the great quarry at Giza, remove one limestone building block and bring it back to the land of your birth. We shall then ordain you Mak of Nuba."

The second Elder then bowed and handed the stick to Uncle Remus, an old man with gray hair cropped atop his ears and a white beard formed his chin, he looked every bit the portrait of wisdom. It was rumored that Uncle Remus was known to have mysterious traveling abilities which allowed traveling in time.

It was said that once, while gallivanting in the future, Uncle Remus found himself surrounded by cotton fields, in a place where cotton was considered King. For Remus, the cotton lacked any semblance of royalty and to him "King Cotton" was an oxymoron. He wasted no time exiting the cotton fields.

Still intrigued by the future, Uncle Remus settled in a cave high in the Caucus Mountains. A short lived hibernation however, when he noticed (for lack of sunshine) the whitening of his skin. Uncle Remus was beginning to look more like a paper towel "Mister Kleen" rather than a Slam Dunk" Mister Shaq. This did not forte well for Uncle Remus, so he hurried up and got "dem bones" out of "dem caves" now he is *black* in the sunny past.

Uncle Remus address Erastus, "Son of Nuba, for your ship crew we offer 100 men; and for their comfort we offer 101 women. The one woman of which I speak is our pride and joy, Jamiama, a leader among women who will provide invaluable assistance in maintaining peace aboard your vessel, and at some point you shall discover her tasty sweet bread.

"Also one of our most tested warriors 'Lil black Sambo' has also asked permission to join your crew. He is the first to come forward and will no doubt courageously blaze your trail. If you accept the offer, I shall inform him.

"Your ship will be finished in 480 days and will be placed upon smoothly carved rolling logs. The rolling logs shall be set upon evenly-spaced parallel logs which track northward. This is to ensure you understand the difficulties of sailing a ship on dry land. Choose whatever else you may need, my son." Uncle Remus then broke the talking stick in half and dropped both pieces to the ground, a time honored gesture indicating the last word had been spoken.

Erastus gathered his crew and instructed them to follow Sambo's dictates. Sambo ordered tree-chopping crews to clear pathways and then formed a gang of ox-handlers, each of which was assigned one ox as a work companion and was held responsible for its performance. Another group was assigned ox-hitching duties. Now the oxen's job was to pull the barge forward across the rolling logs as the crew retrieved the logs from the stern and replaced them at the bow as needed. If the wind was favorable, sails made of stoutly platted vines would assist. Women prepared food on board while others walked alongside carrying water. That day, in front a strong wind and sixteen oxen at tow, Erastus' vessel moved slowly north from the hills of Bilued el-Sudan.

When out of site, sly Sambo blazed a trail ending at the banks of the River Nile. Needless to say, sailing a ship on dry land was short lived.

CHAPTER #3
MAN KNOW THYSELF

Sailing down the Nile, Erastus found many riverside dwellers eager to follow him, most of which had watercrafts. When finally arriving in the lower valley, his group had many smaller boats which were all filled to capacity. Erastus walked far into the valley's lush growth. He tarried awhile before coming back out.

The following day, a very pleased leader stood before his people.

"It has been many years since we departed our beloved Nuba. During the perilous journey, our numbers have increased 100 fold; villagers joining us and birth of children have strengthened our resolve, and I believe the valley before us is reward for our unbending toils; therefore, we shall not return home. God has planted us here and here we must stay. Now proceed to the four corners of this valley and set your camps."

Centuries passed, and the Nile valley provided everything needed for Nuba survival. It was hard work transforming the vast Oasis into a horn of plenty. The labor wasn't all bad as the busying kept everybody occupied which helped avoid most internal strife. The production of food became commonplace and necessitated a bartering system that kept greed and hoarding at a minimum.

First, Erastus issued a decree of disbursement which declared all essentials such as food, shelter, tools, and hospitality services to remain under the control of the hierarchy. Craftsman, however, were permitted to barter wares if they were constructing or inventing something which would benefit the dynasty's survival. Items of luxury were permitted in the bartering system as long as the African adage of "fairness is the best policy" prevailed. The Minister of Barter resolved all disputes and issued harsh punishment to those who did not comply. It was a worthy system which denied gifted people dominion over others, and the arrangement contributed greatly to peace. Nuba of southern Sudan had arrived at the right place and right time for the shift toward civilization. The leadership of boy-Erastus destined him as *Pharaoh Erastus, the First.*

The Erastus Dynasty endured for 1,000 years, and although chance had a part it was not fundamental for survival. Erastus the First wisely envisioned that any undisciplined successor would allow all sorts of trickery from those opportunistic enough to seek unworthy favors. So he etched in stone edicts of law, principles for leaders to live by that did not allow frailty of human nature to threaten the dynasty's survival.

The primary acts of the Pharaoh, Edict #1: Choose a proper mother for the Pharaoh's children. Ensure the woman is of sound mind, physically strong without afflictions, commands a well-purported stance, and possesses movements which are graceful and pleasing to the eye. However, and above all else, her attraction to Pharaoh must be affectionate, rather than lust for status.

Edict #2: A reigning monarch must sire only two sons. Both are to receive leadership training, but the first holds the birthright to the throne. In addition, a vow of celibacy must follow the birth of a second son, providing the eldest was in good health. This restriction accordingly eliminated any false claims to the bloodline.

Erastus the First was quite aware of the difficulties set forth in the edicts nonetheless he believed success with such a challenging task gave credence to a leader's exalted wisdom. He believed this to be an essential gift for those whose decisions were trusted and obeyed so readily.

The science of agriculture set in place by Erastus the First was steadfast. Fields of grain covered the valley's floor in every direction with thick, fruity orchards between. A massive irrigation system steadily flowed, ensuring crops never thirsted. Animals were domesticated and collected for every conceivable use and horses bred massively. During harvest time, the smell of fried chicken and roasted grain permeated the entire valley.

Erastus the Second and Third reigned and passed, and by 4670 B. C., Erastus the Third erected the dynasty's first palace on the slope of a small mountain which rested close to the Nile. The structure so pleased him, he decreed every 3rd Pharaoh after him should construct an exact replica further upslope. The purpose behind building further up the mountain was because it was an excellent vantage point of the thriving valley, and Erastus the Third wanted to make sure his successors didn't lose sight of what kept them fed. The view also focused on the Nile. Snaking northward with the sun glaring on its surface, it awakened the eye and mind to the presence of omnipotence; reminding all to keep the faith.

Erastus the Fourth now held the whip and scepter. He was an academic known affectionately as "the writing Pharaoh." He had little interest in day-to-day decision making and delegated his authority to make time for the passion of philosophy, his first love.

During his tenure, different schools of thought appeared, fostered by one dominant vision *"Man, Know Thyself."* It is difficult to imagine that a stronger directive for thinking truthfully could emerge that far back in antiquity. Similarly, the philosophic doctrine of *"Summum Bonum"* was developed, teachings that strengthened one's self-control.

Summum Bonum, according to C.H. Vail's "Ancient Mysteries" and professor George G.M. James' "Stolen Legacy," was the foundation of virtues, such as fairness, temperance, fidelity, etc. which helped cultivated self-control by holding man's evil, lustful side in subordination and allowed his good and loving side to flourish. The doctrine of Summum Bonum was a way of life which Amarna propagated by one telling themselves the truth.

In 4370 B.C., discovery of arithmetic had enhanced the sphere of life for Amarna. Applied numbers improved proficiency in architecture as well as crafts. Workshops appeared in villages, making tools and weapons plentiful; and the use of numbers also unlocked access to the law of opposites.

Six centuries later, Erastus the Tenth took the throne. His skin was dark, and his features chiseled as though from granite rather than born of a woman. He was medium height, thick and muscular, and had close-cropped hair. He looked every bit a native son however shadowed by a curse. During his upbringing, teaching ministers predicted Erastus the Tenth would create a "fork in the road" for the Erastus' Dynasty. True to prediction while watching the construction of his father's palace, young Erastus decided he would not follow Erastus the Third's building dictates.

"My palace shall stand near that summit up yonder," he vowed. And after his father's passing, Erastus the Tenth wasted little time erecting his luxurious abode. Sounds of axes shaping limestone blocks, mixed with grunts of straining men, echoed the proof that important work had begun. And after the final colonnade was paved and workers good bye waved a rust-colored palace stood. The four identical structures erected upon Pharaoh's Mountain displayed the dynasty's scepter, and distracted not least of beauty that was Valley of River Nile's.

This is indeed a view from top, thought Erastus the Tenth as he strolled on a balcony overlooking his domain. How generous of my ancestors, to position me so that I might peer down and gain inspiration from their ascending spirits.

As the Pharaoh gazed off into the distance, his eyes passed over the architectural achievements and garden retreats left to him from each passing generation. His eyes rested on a grove of high-swaying palm trees which marked his grandfather's sprawling resort complex, known as The Recluse of Min, named after his grandfather's architect.

Erastus the Tenth is heir to a domain which stretched far beyond his seat in the Nile Valley, his influence reached north to the Mediterranean Sea. In those earlier times, the Red Sea delayed the dynasty's eastward advance, so Pharaoh's armies went south into tropical Africa in search of spices, workers, and other spoils. To the west, Erastus' Dynasty controlled Sahara's gold and salt trade routes, as well as other links across the vast Sea of Sand. Often time, Pharaoh's soldiers were seen camped at a far out oasis, sprinkling salt on sweet watermelon to help combat the intense heat, an ancient desert survival technique which remained misunderstood for centuries.

"From here to Timbuktu is a long way. If you gonna cross that 'Sea of Sand,' ya better drop some of that *'nub'* (original name for gold) and take more salt with you boy." Was advice constantly offered.

Erastus' Dynasty was also an empire requiring many government departments. Each of the six provinces was governed by their own priest. Masonry structures teemed with ministers who were charged with serving citizens' needs and all answered only to Pharaoh. The war minister appointee assured control of the militia and all conquered territories. In the valley of the River Nile, none other than mighty Pharaoh uttered the last word of authority.

Official meetings were held in the gathering hall in the lower level of Erastus' palace. An entrance vestibule led into the sizeable room. It was a majestic hall which flaunted circular staircases crawling up the wall. At the far end of the hall's interior, sat Pharaoh's Throne. Openings and skylights were constructed to allow proper lighting, and as if done intentionally, the lighting proudly highlighted the throne. There was mass seating lined five rows deep on both sides of the center aisle. This was to ensure everyone faced Pharaoh.

In ancient Egypt, society was structured in a manner to move a civil way of life forward, and as always something conjured the mix. Case in point, the "fork in the road" prediction leveled at youthful Erastus began to rear its ugly skull. Pharaoh Erastus the Tenth didn't accept mistakes from department heads and considered failure a personal affront. Those in ministerial positions who had failed expectations were offered two choices: resign and become a servant or remain with hope of redemption. A second failure, however, offered no such forgiveness. A palace surgeon anxiously waited for all who failed his Sovereign twice. By Pharaoh's decree, the good doctor would remove the minister's genitals expeditiously. Consequently, it was rare indeed for anyone to fail Erastus the Tenth a second time. Most ministers believed putting up family jewels for the second chance was simply not worth any potential benefits.

Once during a gathering, five head ministers faced Pharaoh. All had come to naught in performance of duty. When Erastus offered alternatives, each minister bowed, grabbed his genitals and in single file did a Michel Jackson moon walk towards an exit. A "fat Albert" look-a-like bringing up the rear lost rhythm, stumbled, and while still clutching his vitals, managed a balancing act while falling out the opening. The gathering hall roared with laughter that day.

On the other hand, Osro the agriculture minister was "split from a different stump." Accused of allowing floodwater to wash away 1,000 pomegranate trees, he stood before the Pharaoh and asked for a second chance.

"My Lord Pharaoh," Osro exclaimed, "my failure was aberrant and with your permission, I choose to remain at my post."

"So be, it," replied Erastus, "but before you leave, Minister, give me a report on the grain harvest for the coming year."

"Oh wise and generous Pharaoh; one who feeds our hungry mouths and quenches our parched thirst, I assure the harvest shall be plentiful this year. Already, your vast fields are surpassing last year's yield by two fold. Do not let a single doubt linger in thy mighty mind or one sleepless night disturb your time of rest, for people of your wondrous land shall feast well this year."

Minister Osro was wrong. For at that very moment, an innumerable swarm of locusts descended on the entire grain crops and blanketed the fields. Pharaoh Erastus summoned his agriculture minister.

Osro arrived and stood before the Monarch with humbleness. Arising from his seat Erastus peered down at Osro with eyes so fixed it caused him to tilt backwards.

"What have you to say for yourself, Minister?"

"I'm compelled to ask for mercy, Oh Pharaoh. My vision was limited, and I did not imagine the winged insects would be so famished. I ask only for mercy."

"Mercy, you ask for mercy??" Erastus bellowed. "Can I feed multitudes of this land with mercy? Or perhaps this mercy you seek will cast an enchantment on your swarm of locusts?"

"Oh mighty Pharaoh, I have served the dynasty well the last ten years. Have I no standing on which to lean?"

"Minister Osro, "It is not what you usta be wuz, but what you now be is." Guards, remove this minister from my sight and take him to the palace surgeon."

Two guards seized Osro, ushering him down a long hallway as echoed his final plea, "Oh merciful Pharaoh, allow that I might spend one final night with my wife! I have only one offspring, Lord Pharaoh, who is of age and in need of family! Reprieve me a bit of time perchance my final endeavor may bear fruit!"

But his pleas fell on deaf ears for Erastus the Tenth had already adjourned the gathering for that day.

Another day passed in the lower valley of the River Nile. Creeping shades of night replaced the gloaming sun. Work was done and a full moon rose, resisting night's encroachment. The vast valley of the River Nile lay in peace as darkness slackened.

Nevertheless, there was little serenity inside the palace of Erastus the Tenth. Within the confines of his chamber, the Pharaoh sat in deep, reflective thought.

"I am well past the age of puberty yet haven't fathered a son. Am I without essence? Where is my being and where oh where is my elusive soul? I have been steadfast in following the dictates of my ancestors. Should I accept this empty feeling of puppetry for my devotion? I, Pharaoh think not."

Moonbeams pierced into the palace openings, illuminating Erastus' chamber. The eerie brightness halted his thoughts. Erastus rose and strolled onto a balcony, beckoned by the moonlit night. He was without clothes.

With outstretched arms, body basking in the lunar glow, *The Naked Pharaoh* lamented, "I see the moon and the moon sees me. Now, oh moon, enlighten my mind as you have brightened my body. I, Pharaoh, am sovereign to the valley of the River Nile, yet restraints upon my status deny me fulfillment. My sexual desires are stronger than self-control, and the will to resist weakens daily. Even as I speak, oh moon, my loins harden with desire for the naked nymphs often seen frolicking in the River Nile. With every heartbeat my extremities throb, and how relieving it would be to have this lust milked from me. But I am forbidden, so speak, oh bright glowing one, for my wit is at end."

The moon sneaked behind a cloud. Darkness reclaimed the night, and the naked Pharaoh reclaimed his chamber!

An aide silently approached and softly spoke, "Lord Pharaoh, thou who rules the ground on which we walk, the night has fallen and your day tomorrow will be hurried. Allow that I might interrupt your thoughts so your servants and I may attend your needs."

"Hush!" snapped the Pharaoh. "At this moment you're without capacity to serve my needs. Get busy and send messengers to the guardian of the dynasty's edicts. Have them here at sunrise thirty days from now. Make haste, Aide; my patience is limited."

Erastus the Tenth retired that night with thoughts of change for he and his dynasty.

Thirty days later just before dawn, the five priest keepers of the dynasty's edicts arrived and sat quietly, facing Erastus' throne. The Pharaoh entered, acknowledged their greeting, and took a seat.

"From this day forward, I shall not allow Erastus the First to control my sexual urges from the tomb," he admonished. "Therefore, I command you to remove from the dynasty's edict all lettering which hinders my desire to sire, and most certainly that vow of celibacy. It is madness to expect me to pass through life restricted by another's whims. Are there any objections?"

The priests bowed replying in unison, "Your wishes are respected, Oh Gracious One."

Pharaoh Erastus left the gathering hall with quickness.

Heads still bowed, one priest said aloud to his brethren, "Our Pharaoh exudes change, and I believe his edict amendments are past due and righteous. Let us pray that chaos does not

accompany the abruptness of his decision."
Harmony echoed inside the gathering hall that day,
for five priests sang in agreement, "Aaaamen."

News of Pharaoh's decision traveled quickly,
causing new-found joy among the people,
especially the women-folk. Now women of the Nile
had a chance to become mother to a Pharaoh.
Needless to say it prompted quite a bit of shimmy
and shake around that Nile Valley.

Now in addition to the first conscious thought of
arts and science and its application to human
conditions, people of the Nile realized that countless
centuries of civilized development could not endure
without the incitement of "the booty grove" a vital
contribution indeed! Simply, shake, shake and
shake your booty!

CHAPTER #4
THE RECLUSE OF MIN

Harvest time had come upon the Nile Valley. The gathering hall was filled with department heads submitting their annual reports. Pharaoh was sitting quietly, observing all the proceedings, when his newly appointed agriculture minister approached. He promptly asked for an update on the insect eradication plan.

"Lord Pharaoh, we have set all affected fields ablaze. Our torch bearers were quite fortunate with timing as the pests had not yet finished crunching. Their remains add wonderful nutrients to our fields for spring planting."

"And is our stored food sufficient to cover our loss?"

"Yes, Lord Pharaoh. All sectors have reported, and we have an adequate hoard."

"Well done all, this meeting is adjourned."

Pharaoh Erastus felt pleased with his minister's performance. He couldn't remember a time when they appeared so attentive to their duties.

"I must learn the reason for my ministers' new-found energy," he thought. "Aide…"

"Yes Lord Pharaoh…"

"Summon the minister of information and have him in the gathering hall two days from now."

Two days later, Erastus entered the gathering hall, and in front of his throne, he observed a line of stacked tablets. Standing on a pedestal near the tablets was a bald headed, muscle-bound Pygmy dressed in a knee length dashiki. The Pharaoh sat quietly observing the man and then asked if he was the one he had sent for.

"Yes, my Lord Pharaoh, I'm Nnowwo, your Minister of Information." "Very well Nnowwo, it is important for information gathers to know everything about their position, however I am a bit perplexed by the volume of tablets you brought, and why the pedestal?"

"Lord Pharaoh," Minister Nnowwo answered, "I hail from far south of the third cataract, and my people are small in stature. When I learned I must stand before you, I panicked, thinking I'd better bring everything because I can't afford to lose any of my scarce ass; the pedestal adds equality of height while addressing taller constituents."

"Rest assured Minister, your Pharaoh's foot is non-threatening at the moment, but we shall revisit my concerns about that standing-stool later.

"Minister Nnowwo," the Pharaoh began, "recently my department heads were as focused as a swarm of blackbirds deciding pecking order, and I need to know the reason."

"The Recluse of Min, Lord Pharaoh," answered Nnowwo. "As you are aware, your department heads have weighty responsibilities, and prospect of failure shadows them like heel-hounds. Minister Isaiah, the headmaster at Recluse, identified the problems as all work no play and decided their work ethics needed universal balance. Minister Isaiah devised a method to offer rejuvenation, allowing department heads to visit Recluse for rest and recuperation. The program there is extraordinary, My Liege, and it serves your ministers very well."

Erastus stepped down from his seat and walked around Nnowwo, eying the pedestal intently.

"Minister," he lectured, "people of leadership within my dynasty come from all walks of life. Different colors, shapes, and different sizes. There is one thread however that binds us together □ we do not use crutches to gain status." With those words, Erastus kicked at Minister Nnowwo's stool. Before Erastus' foot made contact, Nnowwo pushed off and did a double somersault, landing squarely on his feet. The little man stood tall, as if next to a giant about to fall.

The Pharaoh reclaimed his seat and applauded Nnowwo for his fine presentation. "Breakfast is served, Minister. Will you join me?"

Nnowwo bowed and answered, "Most certainly, Lord Pharaoh. And though your reminder was most unexpected, my own two feet and I shall forever be grateful."

Back in his chamber Erastus again felt a nudging from the past.

"The Recluse of Min huh," he thought. "My grandfather must be getting more comfortable in the hereafter knowing his work is still contributing to the dynasty. I must make further inquiries into what's going on down there.

"Aide…"

"Yes my Pharaoh…" bowed Erastus' aide.

"Dispatch our most speedy messenger to the Recluse of Min and issue a summons to Minister

Isaiah. Have him here at the palace three days from now."

Three days later, Isaiah, the minister from

Recluse arrived. He was a slender man, elderly, medium height, and had burnt copper-colored skin with tightly spun red hair. Isaiah's egg-shaped face was not easy to look upon without smiling. Somebody in his family tree must have "jumped the fence," because Isaiah was both Nuba and something else.

He had been a fixture in the dynasty's hierarchy for years; his quick wit and joviality were always welcomed at gatherings. Erastus the Ninth was especially fond of Isaiah and allowed him lifetime tenure at Recluse. Though Isaiah had served the throne for some time, this was the first time he had ever appeared before Erastus the Tenth.

"Greeting minister, I'm told you and your people have worked miracles upon my staff. How did you accomplish this most appreciated task?"

The minister bowed and returned Pharaoh's salutations.

"It is difficult to explain all we do, Lord Pharaoh. Suffice it to say, our goal is to free one's mind, body, and soul of burdens which hinder quality of life. Woman Toui, the high priestess and superior to Recluse, directs our staff. She is astute with clear insight into the influences of fatigue. Under her leadership, all who enter our house depart with a renewed zeal for life. Governor Kumen of Province Four, is a frequent visitor, and can attest to our efficiency, Lord Pharaoh."

"That won't be necessary, Minister. My department head's newfound devotion honors you, and I have no further questions. However, woman Toui does interest me. At your convenience, arrange for her to visit me at Pharaoh's Mountain."

"My Lord Pharaoh," Isaiah answered nervously, "if my answer displeases you, might I die a thousand deaths; but the woman Toui is a very private person who does not socialize well. When her work is done, she secludes herself and cares for an ailing loved one. Also, my Pharaoh, it is rumored the woman Toui harbors only disdain for the occupants of Pharaoh's Mountain. I, your humble servant, would not relish standing before you after she responded to your request; for her wit is quicker than a hummingbird's flight and her speech is sharper than the bite of an asp. So I beg you–"

"Hush!" shouted the Pharaoh. "Enough, I shall invite the woman myself. Aide, escort Minister Isaiah to where we quarter horses. On the way, have my surgeon introduce himself, and then allow Isaiah two choices of our prized stallions. Minister Isaiah, these gifts are in appreciation of your unmatched service; nevertheless do not refuse your Pharaoh again."

While being escorted toward the stables, after visiting the surgeon's quarters, Pharaoh's aide noticed Isaiah was patting on himself, as if missing something.

Thinking Isaiah was doing The Hambone, a rhythmic leg slapping dance, the aide chimed in and sang, "'Hambone, hambone where ya been; round da kitchen and back again.' I see you as an enthusiast of The Hambone leg slap," remarked the aide.

"Hambone my ass…" replied Isaiah looking back towards the palace… "I'm just making sure that scalpel-slinging doctor didn't sneak up on me."

Though Erastus the Tenth had not fathered a son, he still could not allow himself sexual fulfillment simply for pleasure's sake, changes in the dynasty's edicts notwithstanding. The dictates of ancestors kept him self-denied. When his needs stiffened words like "when in doubt don't" and "know thyself young'n" whispered "uh!" "Uh;" Erastus complied. How long oh mighty Pharaoh before your nature exact fulfillment?

The next day, the sun shined bright, and its warming rays brought laughter and good cheer inside Erastus' palace. The Pharaoh sat alone, but not lonely; gaiety of his people pleased him.

An aide silently approached, "What are your needs, Lord Pharaoh?"

"Bring a cup of juice, and then send a messenger to Recluse of Min. Inform the woman Toui her Pharaoh will arrive noontime in fifteen days. And aide…"

"Yes, Lord Pharaoh?"

"Let it be known that I expect her greetings."

"Oh joy, finally our Pharaoh seeks companionship!" shouted the aide as he rushed to dispatch a messenger.

Calmness settled over Pharaoh's Mountain that evening, and everything lay still. In the distance, storm clouds hovered ominously, waiting their turn to join fray.

On the day of departure, Pharaoh Erastus was exceedingly happy. "Prepare my chariot with white horses," he instructed. "Contrast between the beasts and I must be vivid upon my arrival. Make haste, Aide, your Pharaoh has need for swiftness."

The aides rushed to and fro. Dressed in a purple wrap- around skirt and matching skull cap with gold inlaid sandals, Pharaoh Erastus indeed posed a striking figure. Naked from waist up, his ebony skin contrasted well with the white stallions. The gold cobra emblem protruding from his skullcap proudly displayed boss scepter.

The road down Pharaoh's Mountain was treacherous. Circling in front of each tier of the palace, it arched wide near the edge of cliffs. To Lose control of one's chariot while descending offered no mercy. Erastus the Tenth was well known for his adventurous chariot outings and always descended the mountain at breakneck speed. The mountain's inhabitants would always gather outside to watch their ruler at his horsemanship.

"Here he come Pharaoh" someone shouted!"

And down he came, standing flat footed and sideways, holding tight reins with the horses at full gallop. The fleet-footed animals appeared to sling the trailing chariot around every curve. The sound of leather cracked against horseflesh; the horses tugged low to the ground, straining to gain more speed. The crowd gasped as the chariot wheels skidded along the cliff edges repeatedly, but each time the speedy steeds snatched Pharaoh from harm's way.

Finishing the perilous descent, Erastus then coached his snorting horses into a proud trot, guiding them toward Recluse of Min.

"One day that chariot will fly off the side of this mountain," someone said.

"I hope not," said another.

"Then he best stay home," said a third. A stout woman standing nearby voiced "That fool in that chariot need a bite of big-booty-Trudy."

The entrance to Recluse of Min began with an opening spaced between towering palm trees, the trees being perimeter for the large quadrangle used annually for circus festivities. The closely linked trees converged on both side of twin columns that front Recluse's main building. The columns support rounded stairs that climbed to a large garret and viewing balcony that rest above the entrance way.

Inside the lobby, there were stairs on either side of the main entrance. The lobby's rear exit revealed a spacious man-made oasis, dotted with small service structures amply staffed to accommodate visitors. The soothing quietness left nothing amiss for renewing the human spirit.

News of the Pharaoh's visit spread quickly among the nearby villagers, and they drove in mass to glimpse and offer welcome. The Recluse's front yard teemed, with clowns strolled high on stilts and playfully sprinkled guba dusk above spectators. Acrobats and tumblers practiced their skills levitating with every movement. Fire eaters blew smoke from their lips, and trick riders showed off on horseback solely to please the Pharaoh. Pygmy actors prepared a stage to enact past dynasty exploits. Nuba wrestlers covered themselves in white ash and tied gourds to their torso. The hanging gourds challenged opponents to wrestle and break the gourd; bigger the gourd stronger the challenge. The massive fellows wait their turn to show off in front of Pharaoh. Flutists and harpists played mellow harmony among the gathering while Olatungian drummers maintained the beat.

Arranging the festivities was *"The Woman Toui, High Priestess and Superior to the Recluse of Min."* She was a blue-black woman with tightly woven hair framing an effeminately rounded face. Her wide, slanted eyes and smooth, flat nose fit in pleasing proximity to her soft, perky lips. She is a well-proportioned being, slender but with a look of thickness. Her shapely hips connected with sleek thighs, and her slightly bowed legs gave incredible balance to her stance. On that day, woman Toui stood on the balcony with two aides peering toward Pharaoh's Mountain.

"I see a large cloud of dust way over yonder," spoke an aide.

"I see it also," retorted woman Toui. "Perhaps our omnipotent Pharaoh rides that cloud. Come, let us finish our preparations."

Noontime arrived and woman Toui, dressed in a gold smock with matching sandals, stood on the garret at the entrance to "The Recluse of Min." There she waited for her sovereign, Pharaoh Erastus the Tenth.

Directly overhead, the glaring sun announced Pharaoh's arrival. He slowed his horses to a prance and guided the chariot through trees opening. Thunderous applause greeted Pharaoh as crowds divided allowing passage in full pageantry. Erastus steered toward the waiting Toui, she however *did not stir!*

"Whooa," commanded Pharaoh to his tired and nervous horses; the animals obediently calmed. Erastus dismounted and ascended the steps toward woman Toui.

She greeted, "I'm the woman Toui, high priestess and superior to Recluse of Min, welcome to our house, Lord Pharaoh. How may I serve you?" Pharaoh Erastus didn't answer, and seemed mesmerized by the woman's appearance.

Silence lingered and finally Toui spoke again. "Allow my staff and me to present your agenda, Lord Pharaoh."

Still mesmerized, Erastus mumbled. "So be, it."

As Toui's aides approached, she said, "This is Deserae and Deserate Lord Pharaoh, our most esteemed graduates of "The House of Hathor." Proficient in harmony, dance, sexuality, and use of alcohol, their soft-touching hands have prepared a most stimulating bath for you. After which, with your permission, I shall accompany you on the viewing balcony. Our entertainers are ready and anxious to please, Oh Gracious One."

"So be it" Erastus mumbled!

Deserae and Deserate identical twins offered a new meaning to "double your pleasure." With light, chocolate-colored skin, shaven heads, and piercing brown eyes permanently smiling lips dressed in thigh-length tunics which exposed well-shaped legs strolled in front of Erastus toward an enclosed bathing pool

As Erastus followed their lead, he thought, "I pity the fool that bowed to Erastus the First's sexual dictate. These daughters of Nuba I see around here are strictly stacked to bare sons."

Toui's aides were true to task. When Erastus emerged from the bathing pool, his excitement was most obviously physical, and his abstinence showed. Disallowing imprudence, the Pharaoh relaxed himself, dressed, and he and woman Toui ascended to the balcony. While taking a seat, woman Toui clapped her hands. Cymbals clanged! And the show began.

During the end performance a Nuba wrestler, encircled by entertainers, spun his opponent around, tripped him, and then pinned him stoutly to the ground smashing the opponent's gourd. The massive fellow stood glistening in white ash and triumphantly faced the balcony. Erastus and woman Toui began clapping in tribute as other entertainers bowed.

"It is supper time, Lord Pharaoh, if you will accompany me. I'm certain our food offering shall be most pleasing."

"Lead on woman," replied Pharaoh, still clapping.

Erastus again followed a most wanting creature. Woman Toui's slightly bowed legs and measured steps gave incredible rhythm to her shapely rear.

Her loosely fitting garment could not hold sway, though not overtly enticing but exuded sensuality.

That evening as the sun set, it basked the strolling couple in a reddish glow, casting long shadows, and the slaved silhouettes followed obediently.

"Will Pharaoh require companionship with his nourishing?" asked woman Toui while seating him at exquisitely spread table.

"Only you woman, only you," he replied.

Toui bowed and took her seat. They sat quietly while eating, and when finished, Erastus asked the woman her age.

"I'm 22, Lord Pharaoh."

"Have you ever visited Pharaoh's Mountain?"

"Many times," she answered, "I first saw those magnificent palaces for the first time as a child with my mama. And if I might say so, Lord Pharaoh, they're extraordinary."

"Are you learned in the dynasty's ways?" inquired Erastus.

"Very. I studied the dynasty's edicts quite thoroughly, and if boldness does not offend, I believe your recent changes were quite proper. Your self-denial is well known, but even one as mighty as you cannot long endure such unnaturalness."

Pharaoh Erastus stood and thanked the woman for the welcome afforded him, and asked that she visit Pharaoh's Mountain to join him during his annual hunt.

"As you wish, it shall be most interesting observing you in pursuit of your chosen prey, Lord Pharaoh. Although predator and prey rivalry can be confusing, sometimes I'm never quite sure which is which," she added in a barely audible voice.

A messenger rushed into the chamber. "My Liege, your war minister is waiting for you at the palace. Village Tunica in our northern sector has been raided producing dire consequences. Minster Saabon begs your presence before he acts."

"Very well, we shall leave at dawn. Woman Toui…"

"Yes, Lord Pharaoh…"

"You and I will continue our predator and prey conversation at a later date. Now direct me to my sleeping quarters."

Alone in the sleeping quarters, Pharaoh Erastus did not nod into slumber easily. Woman Toui had aroused a want within him unfamiliar in his life of abstinence.

"The feelings that swell within me are far beyond physical. And that suave, enticing being who calls herself woman Toui – nothing other than her pompous swagger could have forced this humility upon me. I, Pharaoh, command you, woman: Remain absent from my dreams, tonight. Affairs of state summon me, and I must rest."

CHAPTER #5
SIWA OASIS

War minister Saabon was a tall, heavy-set man with burnt-black colored skin and tight, nappy hair. His hair bore a permanent part by a scar, the result of a spear that was launched by a charging native during the conquest of Cush. Saabon's stern look, square jaw, and unblinking eyes contributed to his warrior presence. With war bonnets at his side, he and six deputies marched briskly towards the seated Pharaoh and formed a triangle. Scribes entered, sat, and opened tablets. The congregation was motionless.

"Lord Pharaoh," spoke the war minister, "village Tunica of the northeast sector is in ruins. The dead and wounded are mostly unarmed soil tillers. The 300 strong attackers showed no mercy taking women and children into captivity. Presently, only 200 villagers remains, mostly elderly and little people who escaped into bushes at first blood. I'm told only masonry structures withstood the onslaught, Oh Gracious One." The gathering remained silent, disturbed only by Pharaoh's voice.

"At the moment, I do not entertain graciousness, War Minister!" he shouted. "What is being done for those still alive?"

"Minister Ohoe, the building director, is enroute with 200 masons and accompanied by 300 food-bearers, my liege. It shall be enough to start rebuilding."

"And how are the survivors sustaining themselves, Minister?" inquired Pharaoh Erastus.

"One of our roving security force commanded by war woman Imani had just completed a mission east of Tunica. When her scouts reported the raid, she moved decisively, securing the village. She said her rations are adequate to feed the hungry. Fifteen prisoners were captured during the encounter, and they're being brought to Pharaoh's Mountain Lord Pharaoh."

"The invaders are described as fair-skinned with hair the color of gold. At present, they're moving west toward Oasis Siwa and are burdened with captives which would hinder any quick escape. I ordered Imani to follow at a distance and avoid contact. The hot desert sand and I shall not offer welcome to the feet of these strangers, my liege. I expect them to replenish at Siwa, and then turn north toward the Mediterranean Sea, the only escape possible."

"How soon will the problem be resolved, Saabon?" demanded Erastus.

"With your permission, Lord Pharaoh, Imani's forces shall ensure the gang continues toward Oasis Siwa. They will not engage unless the invaders change course. While Imani stalks the enemy at the rear, we shall compile 100 war chariots, 200 foot soldiers, and 100 archers and quickly march to Siwa, arriving ahead of the plunderers. The Oasis will appear deserted. When night falls, our soldiers shall emerge and seal their fate, my liege."

The Pharaoh stood and gestured his war minister to step forward, "Am I to understand you have no need for me in this battle? He asked.

"As always, Lord Pharaoh, your wishes command me, and I am most gratified by whatever you please. It's your strong leadership that compels me to act swiftly, my liege."

"Very well, Minister. Have the captives incarcerated near Pharaoh's Mountain. I shall await your return with the other unfortunates."

"It shall be done, Lord Pharaoh, with the certainty of a quieted, rising sun."

Back at his headquarters, south of Pharaoh's Mountain, Saabon busied himself dispatching scouts. Recently gathered information put the enemy thirty days out from Siwa; quite enough time to move his forces, as planned. Saabon dispatched twenty chariots in advance to establish direction and directed sentries to man outposts for every two days. Support personal with rations followed the sentries. The caravan, comprised mostly of war-chariots with foot soldiers in tow, planned to move post-to-post and rest only during the night, continuing a torrid pace until they arrived at Siwa. Each outfitted with spear and shield, thick-soled sandals, padded long sleeve blouses, and war bonnets. They were a formidable force that carried deadly blades into battle, and the rhythms to which they fought were even more deadly. It took only four days to put Pharaoh's army on the march, and Saabon rolled his chariot four abreast at a steady gait to ensure his trotting foot soldiers did not lag.

Oasis Siwa was a large watering hole located in the northwest valley and sat in close proximity to Sahara's barren eastern border. In centuries past, Siwa's numerous lakes, ponds, and massive forested area was a hub for travelers. Having palms trees swaying, fruit trees laden, blackberry bushes spreading, and watermelon patches scattered made Siwa a stark reminder of scarcities that lie ahead for travelers bound for Timbuktu. Oasis Siwa was also where a determined hunter could find prey. Birds flocked continuously, offering morsels of nutrient for the blessed and skilled hunter. Oasis Siwa had been a pillar of life for so many. This day, however it was now a death trap – a gaping snare set by war minister Saabon, avenger of the people of Tunica!

Arriving upon Siwa, Saabon's commanders set positions behind clustered foliage inside the Oasis' eastern flank. The archers readied themselves up front and the spear and shields stationed themselves at rear. Saabon's well-hidden chariot force took position at a distance on Siwa's southern perimeter. Now, Pharaoh's army waited!

After seven days, two men on horseback approached from the east. Silhouetted by a rising sun, their long shadow preceded a slow approach. Horse and rider sauntered toward the nearest watering hole. While the horses drank, the riders drew their swords and scanned the landscape, as if expecting an attack. Calmness prevailed. The riders then rode further into Siwa's foliage, scouting as they went. Discovering no threat, the horsemen spurred their mounts back from whence they came. Pharaoh's army *did not stir!*

Just before sunset, a throng of horsemen, foreign to the land, arrived at Siwa with Tunica's captives struggling in front of their columns. Their commander was aware of a dogged pursuit at his rear, so he set defenses on Siwa's eastern perimeter. When darkness fell, the invaders lit bonfires, illuminating night's sky, and settled down to rest.

About midnight, guided by the bonfire, the foot soldiers moved swiftly into position. As archers rained arrows into the enemy's camp, foot soldiers charged into battle. Surprisingly, no yelling emitted from the hand-to-hand combat, only the sound of deadly strikes. At the same time, Saabon launched his chariots, and circled back and forth along the enemy's eastern flank, unleashing deadly arrows as they went. When their quivers emptied or horses fell, driver and archer abandoned their chariots and charged into battle with sword and shield.

When morning came, light of day showed the deadliness of battle. The night before Oasis Siwa shared its many colors with crimson red. Bleeding men lay moaning and groaning. Looking over the scene, Saabon ordered the wounded attended, the dead buried, and prisoners gathered. Suddenly! The sound of neighing horses turned Saabon's attention to the east. Shading his eyes from the quited rising sun, he saw a line of war chariots primed for battle. Somehow during the night Imani's forces had moved upon the enemy's heels. They glared at the battlefield anxiously!

CHAPTER #6
DODGING SLUNG ARROWS

Back at Recluse of Min, Minister Isaiah gathered his staff and offered praise for the outstanding welcome presented to Pharaoh.

"I'm pleased to see you all, myself included. My visit to Pharaoh's Mountain left some doubt whether I would be standing here, today. The Pharaoh's hospitality included a threatening introduction to his palace surgeon however the good doctor will have to wait another day for me to become prey. Again, the performance was extraordinary, and many thanks to you all."

Later in the evening, Minister Isaiah explained to woman Toui why he was so conspicuously absent during Pharaoh' visit.

"My meeting with Erastus the Tenth was unnerving for me," he confessed. "The Pharaoh asked for something that was not mine to give, and my response didn't please him. I thought it best not to refresh his memory so soon. Pharaoh Erastus does not offer kindness when displeased."

"I'm quite aware of his ignoble deeds," agreed woman Toui. "And they're as legendary as his self-denial. While he was here, the exalted one asked me to join his annual predator prey exercise, and he appeared determined that I should be among his conquests. So expect me absent from my duties for an extended period."

"Very well woman, go share your particular charm with Pharaoh's Mountain. Inform me before you return so I may prepare a befitting homecoming."

The woman Toui bowed, gave thanks, and took her leave.

From sunup until sundown, the woman Toui practiced. Thirty days later, she arrived at Pharaoh's Mountain with a hunting chariot, Deserae and Deserate, manservants, messengers, cooks, babbaluwa (medicine man), and others. It was a sizeable following indeed for a hunting invite; however unbeknownst to Pharaoh, woman Toui's intent was contrived. By surrounding herself with so many, she knew serenity within Erastus's palace could not withstand the disruptions; and just as intended, they were housed in the palace directly below that of her reigning sovereign.

The pharaoh's mountain's inhabitants gave a warm welcome to the visitors, guiding them about and showing the many attractions. After which the woman Toui chose her sleeping quarters which faced upward toward Pharaoh's favorite balcony. Reclining consciously within Pharaoh's view, she immersed herself in thought.

"Blessed maternity, my instinctive blessed maternity, how thy voraciousness engrosses me. And as if your cravings were not enough, Erastus the Tenth has looked clean through me, kindling desire further. However, time is not in agreement. I know obedience to the spirit of his ancestors cannot reprieve me for long; but until those ghosts from the past concede, perhaps my Pharaoh will appreciate viewing me from afar. I certainly hope so, for it has been said, 'Blacker the berry, sweeter the juice,' a truism most useful for those picking succulent fruits.

"Likewise, as Mama used to say, 'Erected loins which are denied, intensifies desire,' a truism for those desiring black cherries. And I, woman Toui, am most certainly black."

Blackberry bush spread every-which-way,
Clinging with abiding stay;
Anything near bush will embrace,
Blackberry bush grasp without grace;
Know thyself you undisciplined weed;
Your succulent fruit entice plenty greed;
Slow thy role thick thorny stems;
Eager black fingers quit sticking them;
For a thimble of taste pay a prickly price,
Plucking black fruit toss a bittersweet dice

For the big cats roaming the Nile valley, avoiding flying arrows was an annual predicament. Hunting, Pharaoh's favorite past time, and chasing the animals gave rise to a unique method of sport using two-man chariots as the weapon of choice. The pursuit was fast and rewarding, providing vehicles hold together, horses remained true-footed, and arrows hit the mark. Action began when the runner flushed the cats from the surrounding hills onto an open plain. The runners would ensure the frightened animal's only escape route was between two waiting chariots.

When the call bellowed, it indicated a cat was on the way, and the chariots moved forward slowly.

Then, when the cat hit the ground running, it would get caught between the chariots. During the quick encounter, standing archers would try for the kill. More often than not though, the swift felines would elude their pursuers, leaving driver and hunter exhilarated only for the chase.

The hunt duration lasted thirty days or until four kills occurred. Pharaoh's limit was to ensure the animal's survival; but due to the clumsiness of the hunters recently, this was not a problem. Often their only recompense was watching the felines vanish over the horizon.

The woman Toui was no novice at the hunting game; her father had taught her well. Having supper with Pharaoh one night, she informed him of her hunting prowess. Erastus appeared surprised but pleased.

"How many cats have you downed?" he asked.

"During training my arrows was true to mark twice, Lord Pharaoh."

"Again, you impress me, woman. I welcome you to the annual hunt. Your chariot alongside mine shall make a formidable team."

Their conversation paused as servers brought intoxication drink to the table. Erastus began sipping his red elixir and woman Toui hesitantly did likewise.

"Are you promised?" asked Pharaoh abruptly.

"I'm not..." she answered with similar bluntness. "If you will indulge me, I'm one who cannot imagine me as the object of bestowment."

"Have you ever been courted in a mannish manner?" Erastus again asked abruptly.

"My Lord Pharaoh, I am honored and well pleased by the tenor of your queries. They are direct and unassuming which offer me freedom of expression without hindrance. I've never been aroused enough to allow penetration of my being, as I often say. I'm most assuredly virgin."

The Pharaoh stood from his seat, smiled, and asked the woman to stand and face him.

"I beg not, Lord Pharaoh. Your most tasteful drink has warmed me. I'm unaccustomed to its effect. For the moment, I need solitude."

"Your Pharaoh has an abundance of solitude, woman Toui. It would please me immensely to share as much as you need."

The Woman Toui *did not stir!*

"Aide, escort woman Toui home and be especially humble in her presence. You rest well, most tempting one. The hunting starts two days from now and the scent of a woman will add vigor to our proceeding."

Woman Toui stood, bowed, and gave thanks.

Two days later, hunters arrived for the festivities. Some chariots were individually decorated, and one enterprising fellow disguised his horse's face as an antelope – big cat's favorite prey. Day after day, dust rose above the hunting ground and churned skyward from the pounding hooves and speeding chariots. The runners routed more than fifty cats, but not a single one felt the sting of arrows. When the thirty day hunting period came to a close, Pharaoh's team had the honor of the final chase, as was the tradition.

Woman Toui parked her chariot, with the horses poised and ready. Erastus mounted his rig and glanced toward her, nodding his approval. The call bellowed, indicating the prey had been flushed. Both chariots surged forward as a cat drop from the sky between accelerating rigs. Pharaoh's well-trained steeds quickened immediately, and woman Toui's horses kept pace. With an arrow clenched in his teeth and another cocked in the bow, Erastus shot. The feline leapt forward and dodged the dart. Quickly reloading, he shot again and missed. Woman Toui fired an arrow straight, long, and on target; but it fell short, zipping into the ground. The nimble cat sprinted ahead of the tiring horses, and in haste Toui shot again, short. Chariots drivers strike the horses repeatedly but to no avail. The swift feline was long gone, just a spotted blur beyond a cloud of dust!

Erastus' chariot whirled towards the starting line; Toui's chariot followed. Muffled applause greeted the returning teams in appreciation of a gallant try; and as was custom, participators parked side-by-side, awaiting Pharaoh's hunt-ending pass and review ritual. The two chariots passed in front, acknowledging all for effort.

When the last driver wheeled towards home, the archer hollowed over his shoulder. "Lord Pharaoh, next year that big cat with spots on his ass is 'gonna' be mine!"

That evening, Erastus ordered a stout elixir drink. The aide vanished and quickly returned with a large filled goblet.

"Aide, inform the woman who occupies my
father's palace not to leave this mountain until I
dismiss her; and be poetic with your conveyance.
Now leave me."

The aide silently withdrew. Pharaoh Erastus sat
long into the night watching woman Toui prance
through his mind.

"She will most certainly give birth to my sons,"
he said aloud, "and if the chill between us hinder
her willingness, then so be, it." Dizzy from drink,
Erastus nodded into deep slumber.

Quietness prevailed the following two days and
everything was still. On the third day, a messenger
arrived from Saabon.

"The war minister shall arrive in four days with
eighty captives, Lord Pharaoh. I'm to inform you
those combatants who refused to surrender were
interned where they fell, and none of the enemy
escaped, my liege."

"Very well messenger; drink with me." The aide
forced a cup into the frightened messenger's hand.

"Finish the drink son," Erastus encouraged. The
Pharaoh left the room while the messenger drank
his fill.

The following evening, Erastus again invited
woman Toui to supper, and she arrived dressed in a
colorful wrap-a-round skirt with matching halter
and fez.. Fanning leaves in hand and sparkling stone
adorning her navel, well-scrubbed bare feet treaded
softly toward the seated Pharaoh. Erastus sipped his
red elixir and greeted Toui admirably. She bowed
and took a seat.

They began eating in silence until Erastus' voice broke the spell.

"The hunt was especially contentious this year. I hope our aggressive instincts excited you as well, woman."

"It did indeed, Lord Pharaoh. I tried to represent myself desperately as a huntress, but the big cat that went by us during the final chase was quite opposed to any intentions of mine."

Erastus sipped from his cup. "Those damned cats are getting faster and smarter," he quipped. "I sensed high intensity during the final chase. I expected such then, but now the hunt has ended so why do you remain intense, woman?"

"I have feelings within that hinder wholeness, my liege..."

"What? What??" shouted Erastus!

"I am a 22 year old woman unwilling to submit to motherhood."

"Unwilling?" Erastus repeated, again raising his voice. "You, whom *God* has created to bare sons and you are unwilling."

Erastus drank his cup empty, stood, chucked it to the floor, and ordered Toui to stand and face him. The woman did as told. Both stared neither blinked.

"Woman, I'm Erastus the Tenth, sole ruler of the Nile valley and beyond, sovereign to the ground on which you stand and I need sons, and you woman shall give them birth. Now return to your palace. You cannot avoid such as I."

Pharaoh Erastus marched out. Woman Toui remained composed. She poured a drink, finished it, and then asked an aide to escort her home.

CHAPTER #7
SAABON

War minister Saabon with two of his deputies marched briskly toward the seated Pharaoh. The gathering hall filled that day all anxious to hear war news. Stopping in-step, the trio bowed greetings.

"You returned with all of your hair this time, Saabon. Does that mean your mission was successful?"

"I welcome your humor, Lord Pharaoh. It adds semblance to an otherwise dreadful affair, although I do part with my hair rather begrudgingly these days. The mission has been accomplished," Saabon answered soberly. "Imani has returned to Tunica with all but eight hostages, and workers are rapidly repairing dwellings as well as restoring infrastructure. Food-bearers arrived timely and are helping soldiers prepare the fields for spring planting. Your minister of hospitality is also there attending the wounded. All is as well as can be in Tunica, my Lord Pharaoh."

Erastus sipped from his cup, "And how many casualties, Minister?"

"Regrettably we lost thirty-seven. The enemy was well armed with superior weapons, my liege."

"Superior weapons, how so Saabon?"

A soldier came forward, cradling a long, heavy sword. The Pharaoh grasped the weapon, pointed it, and flipped the handle to check its balance.

"As you can see, the blade is heavy and hard with a very sharp edge. Our soldiers fought gallantly against it."

"Can we duplicate this blade?"

"Not at this time, Lord Pharaoh. The substance is iron, and I'm mystified by its durability in battle. Our shields crumbled at first strike."

"Now tell me about our uninvited guest, Minister."

"We have a total of ninety-five captives, my liege, with three claiming peaceful intent."

"Peaceful intention while in the middle of a fight? You must explain this, Saabon."

"The three were captured with the first at Tunica. But I'm told, unlike the others, they were seen assisting our wounded."

Pharaoh Erastus took another sip from his cup. "What are your thoughts concerning the so-called peaceful three?"

"Their hands are not calloused like a warrior's but instead are softer than doctor's cotton. They carried tablets and marking sticks but not weapons. Their actions lend me to believe what they say, my liege."

"Did they arrive before the murderers?"

"All arrived at the same time, my liege. But they mentioned that traveling in search of knowledge offered few choices."

Pharaoh Erastus took one last drink, stood with sword in hand, and spoke directly, "Saabon, a pack of wild dogs attacks distinctly, and my people here have been bitten. There shall be retribution. If your peaceful three are scholars, as you so believe, they shall be crucified, for scholars should endeavor to lead, not just follow."

Saabon bristled! "Lord Pharaoh, I have boundless respect for your leadership, and therefore I assume the right to disagree. Unfairness breeds evil among God's creation. Those trusted with leadership who indulge in such barbarism barters away our existence. That history lesson is clear and unequivocal."

The Pharaoh said nothing, and Saabon continued, "And in defense of my impertinence, may I remind you of Summum Bonum teachings, my liege."

Pharaoh Erastus pointed the sword towards Saabon and shouted, "You are insolent minister!" The congregation groaned! Erastus dropped the sword and left the gathering hall.

Erastus the Tenth was steadfast to his curse. Two days later, the three scholars were crucified on the roadside leading towards the Recluse of Min. During the nights, Erastus sat alone, drink in hand. With each passing day, another prisoner was crucified. After ten days of the carnage, woman Toui received a message from war minister Saabon requesting a meeting as soon as possible. Late one night, a chariot spirited her away, incognito.

The chariot moved swiftly through the night, arriving hastily at army headquarters. Guards waved the gliding vehicle through the main gate, directing it down a long torch-lit road lined with masonry structures. It was Pharaoh's military compound and responsible for vanquished foes for centuries. The woman Toui, high Priestess and superior from the Recluse of Min, found herself approaching Saabon's bureau and living quarters. She was at midst of the deadly blades that behest Erastus dynasty.

A guard escorted Toui inside the main building. Saabon, standing behind a lectern, asked her to seat, and she obliged but declined the offered refreshments.

The war minister spoke bluntly, "I'm told the Pharaoh has chosen you to give birth to his sons. Are you in the family way?"

"No Minister, I'm not," replied Toui tersely.

"A curse rise over our homeland woman, brought on by our Pharaoh seeking vengeance rather than fairness. He is intoxicated with drink and consumed by desire. The crucifixion of prisoners is a crime against God and man. The bloodletting has wiped the smiles off our people's faces and drained laughter from their hearts; you woman are in a position to end the madness. If your selfish unwillingness continues, it shall burden me to act militarily. His is a diminishing lineage that must be preserved.

"I am War Minister Saabon, defender of the Nile valley and beyond, subordinate only to Pharaoh, himself. So allow me a bit of bluntness: Go drop your skirt, and give the boy what he needs."

Woman Toui *did not stir*. Silence lingered. Saabon gestured impatiently for a response.

Finally woman Toui stood and bowed. She looked Saabon squarely in eyes and said, "I shall relieve you of the burden, Minister."

Pleased that he successfully negotiated with woman Toui, Saabon called out, "Guard...Escort woman Toui home, and make certain she is well-cloaked so peeping eyes do not recognize her."

Twelve days had passed since the first crucifixion. On day thirteen, woman Toui requested an audience with Pharaoh. She arrived and found him on a balcony peering toward the Recluse of Min.

Standing slightly behind him, she spoke softly. "Lord Pharaoh, are there any words which I may speak to give you pause to stop these crucifixions?"

"Why should I?" asked the Pharaoh as he looked off coldly toward the horizon.

"I can only offer a heartfelt admission of guilt, Lord Pharaoh. After your visit to Recluse and for personal reasons, I decided to do everything within my power to entice your trust. My intent was so focused I did not consider all its ramifications. Because of my selfishness, the people of the Nile suffer. So I must accept responsibility for the silence of laughter I hear."

"Your concern for the people does not rescue me from myself, woman. The vengeance I crave is out of control, and what's more is I like it. What else do you have to say?"

"The celestial bodies are in alignment, Lord Pharaoh; and our people need festivity not tribulations." She sighed, lifted up her chin, and said, "So I consent my mind, body, and my soul for the birth of our child."

"For what price, woman? And before you answer, advise yourself. I have eyes everywhere and did not sanction Saabon's interference. His deed was impertinent; and upon your arrival, I was contemplating my war minister's fate. So chose your words carefully." Erastus said, clutching his cup.

"If nurturing my well-being offends the Pharaoh, then my time has come and I accept my fate..."

Pharaoh Erastus said nothing and woman Toui continued, "In a far corner at the Recluse sits an edifice. It is the shrine of *"The Sacred Bark of Karnak,"* a place for quietness and prayer. On moonlit nights, I often time seclude there with thoughts of my first lover. To conceive my firstborn under glow of that full moon would be most blissful. When his smile greets the morning sun, my price will be paid, Lord Pharaoh."

"Very well; dreams are without consequence; nevertheless from this day forward, consider your body a haven only for my sons. You may return to your beloved recluse. I shall join you there the first night of a full moon."

Woman Toui bowed, gave thanks, and silently withdrew.

"Aide..."

"Yes, Lord Pharaoh?"

"Send a message to my minister of prisons, and command him to halt and remove all crucifixions. Inform him the sentence for the leader is execution. Have it done without delay, and send all others to the rock quarry at Giza."

"At once, Lord Pharaoh," replied the aide.

The woman Toui wheeled her chariot toward Recluse of Min with her whip held high. Her whip echoed off the mountain as it struck the horse's rump. The mountain inhabitants lined the roadside and waved goodbye, showing appreciation to her. Watching her departure from a balcony, Erastus the Tenth sipped from his cup.

True to his word, Pharaoh Erastus arrived at Recluse of Min the night of a full moon, and Toui's aides escorted him to the enclosed bathing pool near the shrine of "The Sacred Bark." With soft touching hands, Deserae and Deserate prepared him for his engagement with woman Toui, who secluded herself in wait. Woman Toui reclined comfortably on cushioned pallets with feathered pillows tossed about.

Blackness of night deepened, challenging the high-hanging moon to shine brighter. *"The Naked Pharaoh,"* hand-in-hand with aides, entered the Shrine of Sacred Bark. As Deserae and Deserate withdraw, Toui disrobed and welcomed Erastus with outstretched arms, trembling at his touch. Erastus lifted the woman, gently kissing her harden breasts, and eased onto the pallet. Toui spread and Erastus eased his throbbing extremity inside her,

She gasped with pain then with pleasure. Looping one leg over Erastus, Toui tightened herself around his groin. With one hand cradling his head and the other feeding him breast, woman Toui nursed Erastus as a suckling baby, while he stoutly took her virginity. A bright, full moon basked the couple in lunar glow as they danced rhythmically.

Later, Deserae and Deserate returned with cooling drinks for the exhausted lovers. Erastus drank a red elixir while Toui sipped juice. Just before dawn, the aides returned again, awakening woman Toui and escorting her away. Erastus the

Tenth *did not stir!* Come sunrise, the recluse's staff discovered Pharaoh Erastus was dead! "A tremendous strain on his heart," the death report concluded.

Two days passed and under cloudy skies, the funeral caravan arrived and collected Pharaoh's remains; amidst rolling thunder. Wailing villagers! Lightning flashed and pouring rain depart, leaving behind the crescendo of a mournful symphony never before heard in the Nile valley!

Erastus the Tenth's sarcophagus was placed in state near the summit of Pharaoh's Mountain. Day after day, people climbed Pharaoh's Mountain to view his remains.

The sudden demise of such personage heaped widespread sorrow upon the land; and after proper respect was shown, Pharaoh Erastus the Tenth was laid to rest in his father's tomb near Pharaoh's Mountain.

Sixty days later, five priests, keepers of the dynasty's edict, summoned woman Toui to Pharaoh's Mountain. The dynasty's edicts directed the five to jointly assume leadership under such circumstances and to fill the vacancy expeditiously. The purpose behind the priests making the decision was based on trust. Never before in the dynasty's history have priest militias involved themselves in conspiracies. However transfer of power was to be done without delay to disallow organized opportunists a chance to gain power.

The gathering hall was crammed again as people were anxious to see who they would answer to. Woman Toui arrived and sat, facing the five priests.

"Are you with child?" the first priest asked.

"I am," Toui answered.

"Was the conception witnessed?"

"Yes," she replied.

"By whom?" a second priest asked.

Deserae and Deserate stepped forward and bowed. A third priest then asked, "Is there anyone here denying woman Toui's claim?"

No one answered so the third priest ordered woman Toui to stand and accept the Whip and Scepter, symbols of dominance.

Standing with Whip and Scepter in hand, woman Toui crossed her arms against her bosom, signifying rite of power. This power was invested by Erastus the First's edict which states, "If a Pharaoh passes suddenly without an apparent heir, the woman who carries his child shall become sole heir to his throne." So it is scribed, so shall it be. And so it was.

Toui the First wasted little time consolidating power. The woman Pharaoh summoned all department heads to council and after three days of wrangling all acceded to her demands.

Minister Saabon, being subordinate only to the Pharaoh himself, did not attend; for his discussions required privacy. Later when confidence increased, the Woman Pharaoh ordered her war minister to stand before her.

Minister Saabon arrived and, as practiced, marched briskly towards the seated Pharaoh. He stopped, bowed, and offered greetings.

Pharaoh Toui acknowledged the greeting, stood, pointed at Saabon and said softly, "You may kneel, Minister."

"I kneel only to strengthen faith, Lord Pharaoh," Saabon replied tersely.

"Very well, Minister. I didn't expect one such as you to grovel easily. My father spoke admirably of courageous deeds, and your posture here attests that gallantry. He also mentioned misgivings you had with Erastus the Tenth, problems forcing you into the military service. Would you care to elaborate?"

"It was a personal matter, my liege. I chose to let it rest."

"Then we shall let it be, Minister, but I shall require the same loyalty afforded Erastus the Tenth."

"I stand ready, my Pharaoh," Saabon said, bowing.

"Then you're dismissed."

Saabon turned about and started toward an exit.

"Saabon!" voiced the Pharaoh.

Saabon stopped, turned, and again faced Pharaoh.

"During our prior meeting, I became embarrassed by your choice of words. I assume your vulgar outburst was out of character and was brought on by loyalty concern. Nevertheless, it would greatly behoove you to not trespass on my sensitivities again."

"With humbled assurances, oh mighty Pharaoh," replied Saabon.

Seven months later, the woman Pharaoh, Toui the First, one and only child of disgraced agriculture

minister Osro, gave birth to a nine pound boy, and
he is by deed "split from a different stump"
Pharaoh Erastus the Eleventh.

Pare not rind us nurturing need,
severed seed impede life breed,
indeed, indeed,
take heed.

CHAPTER #8
THE WOMAN PHARAOH

Toui the First remained close to Pharaoh's Mountain during the baby's first six years, a minding mama while learning the responsibilities of leadership. During the official gathering when she hesitated or appeared indecisive, department heads respectfully offered advice, enhancing loyalties.

With each passing day, the woman Pharaoh gained more confidence and began examining past dynasties' decrees that were contrary to her upbringing. The most important being the unholy alliance between Erastus the Tenth and his palace surgeon which disgraced her father. That dastardly deed had moved woman Toui towards vengeance, and she devised a plan to gain a high position of trust so she might enact deadly revenge on those responsible. Pharaoh's hunting invitation simply made things easier. Now though, woman Toui was Pharaoh Toui the First; a leadership position that was better than any thirst for revenge. She could not allow the deadly 'eye for an eye' code to *blind* her leadership.

Yet Toui's grief lingered and craved soothing. The palace surgeon, who had disappeared, was finally found and brought naked before her on bended knees.

"My father suffered much because of you, scoundrel," Toui told the frightened surgeon." "Though he died peacefully with forgiveness in his heart, I, his only daughter, am not so forgiving." With those words, Toui stepped from her throne,

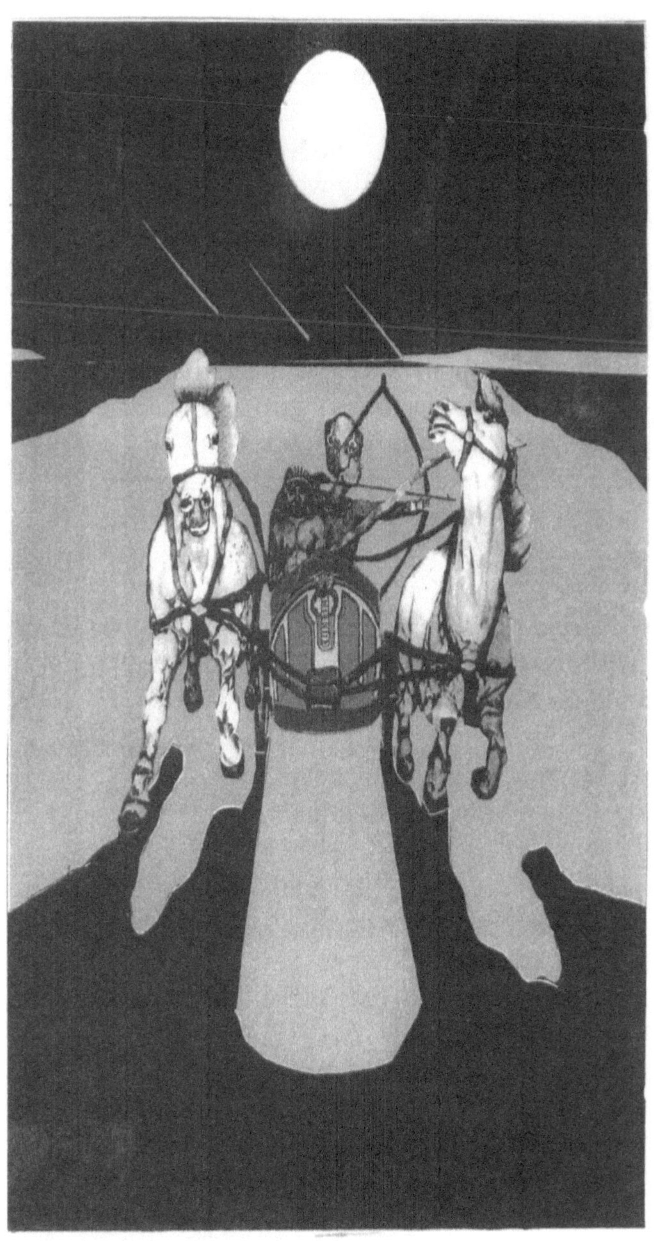

hooked the scepter around the surgeon's neck, and began cracking her whip across the cowering surgeon.

"Your bloody deed is no longer welcome here," Toui said, speaking softly while striking him unmercifully.

As the surgeon screamed, his painful cry echoed down the same hallway Toui's father voiced *his* final plea. The Whip and Scepter, symbols of Pharaohs' dominance were wielded that day.

After the final lash, the guards hustled the quivering surgeon outside, loaded him on a chariot, and unceremoniously dropped him at bottom of Pharaoh's Mountain.

During an evening supper, Deserae and Deserate suggested to the woman Pharaoh she should travel about the valley.

"Meeting and greeting people is a sound way to display your reign," they advised.

"A sound idea, I will think about it. Now send in my son."

The aides withdrew as boy Erastus entered.

"Hi Booboo," Toui cooed, "How would you like to go far away with Mama?"

"Maama," the baby cried. Toui lifted and hugged him tightly.

Pharaoh Toui took the aides' advice. On the day of departure, dressed in a gold colored blouse, wrap-around skirt, and matching skull cap, the woman Pharaoh presented a most eye-pleasing monarch.

"Is the caravan ready?" she asked.

"Yes, my liege. Loaded and awaiting you and your son at bottom of this Mountain."

"Strike the horse then, Captain; and let's be gone."

Whack! The whip sounded; twin white horses lurched forward, prancing down the mountain's winding road.

A company of horse soldiers led the caravan, followed by two war chariots. Pharaoh's specially built chariot was next in line ahead of the well-decorated staff's vehicles. Elephants, camels, oxen, and other beast of burdens that were laden with supplies took their places. Out-riders guarded both the right and left flanks while a company of horse soldiers brought up the rear. Toui the First was on a quest to greet her people impressively. The colorful caravan aided her will.

Forward messengers had instructed each governor to welcome everyone at Pharaoh's gatherings. Many cheerfully obliged. The only antagonist was governor-priest Kumen, grandfatherly boss of province four. Unbeknownst to Pharaoh, Kumen had a tight relationship with war minister Saabon and visited the army headquarters quite regularly.

Kumen's' indifference toward the woman Pharaoh surfaced during their first meeting, causing her to extend her stay and engage him further. He displayed aloof politeness in her presence, answering her questions short and curtly without elaborations.

During one conversation, his attitude so irritated
the Pharaoh she ordered him to bow and remain
silent. Kumen, not being use to such subservience
from women, did not comply and stood defiant.
Pharaoh's guards stepped forward and banged their
spear handles on the floor! Governor Kumen got the
message and capitulated.

Pharaoh Toui did not like Kumen, and liked him
even less when she was informed he controlled a
fleet of barges that sailing the Nile.

Nevertheless, the woman Pharaoh made many
new friends during her travel. Now she better
understand the importance of having the trust of the
people; moreover, she is aware of which den her
enemy lie. On the way back home Toui felt
humbled and gave thanks.

"Welcome home, Lord Pharaoh" spoke the
gathered staff as she stepped from the chariot.

Toui smiled at the welcome and said, "I am glad
to be back home. This mountain has never looked
so good, not to mention all your beautiful smiles."

"You're home indeed," replied her captain.

"Many thanks to you all," said Toui." All bowed
and slowly withdrew.

A glowing sunset brightened Pharaoh's
Mountain that evening, basking Toui as she sat on
her favorite balcony. Having a need for
companionship she asked for her masseur, a body
builder name Ed-tutn-Nut. He was an uncanny
fellow, brought from Recluse of Min for his
extensive knowledge of pain. Pharaoh Toui needed
him to ensure her staff remained physically fit,
among other things.

Ed-tutn-Nut believed laughter and smiles healed, and he forced the treatment on all he served. "Whom, why, for, and because" was his questioning mantra, and his clients' response often brought forth laughter. Ed-tutn-Nut also used his philosophy as justification for personal eroticism. Although sometime vulgar, his mental prowess kept him in life's place. The staff's healthy appearance and lively performance attested his abilities, and on rare occasions she indulged herself. After the exhausting trip this night, woman Pharaoh felt well obliged.

A short time later, captain of the guard informed Pharaoh Toui that governor Kumen had gone to army headquarters and demanded her rise to power be investigated. War minister Saabon complied with the demand and ordered the attendants who first discovered Pharaoh's body, as well as minister Isaiah, the palace surgeon, Deserae and Deserate and all to report to army headquarters.

Intense questioning lasted for days. After which Saabon released all except the palace surgeon. Still visibly frightened by his encounter with Pharaoh, he requested tenure in the army far from Pharaoh's Mountain. Amused by the surgeon's fears, the request was granted.

The report concerning Isaiah's questioning gave a more dishonorable account, and when informed of her former boss's treatment, Toui the First became angry; however she said nothing.

CHAPTER #9
WAR WOMAN IMANI

The woman Pharaoh felt pressured; there were forces positioning for power within as well as outside the hierarchy. Toui summoned visors to assess the situation.

"The dynasty's edict ensures your control over the provinces, my liege; and your department heads remain loyal, although we hear grumbling from within the army," they told her.

The woman Pharaoh strolled onto a balcony and scornfully said to no one in particular, "I will bring ruin to any wishing to disrupt the Erastus' Dynasty. Aide, send a message to war minister Saabon and order him and his staff to the gathering hall in forty days."

Forty days later, war minister Saabon arrived in his usual manner. He and nine commanders marched lock-step toward the seated Pharaoh. Saabon's deputies were so similar in appearance with their oval faces, thick bodies, and dark as ebony, they all could have all been twins. Holding feathered bonnets stoutly, their warrior demeanor portrayed little doubt these men were the guardians of the Nile valley. Stopping in unison, the group nodded respectfully.

"Welcome back Lord Pharaoh," spoke Saabon. "It's good to have you home,"

"I'm pleased to see you as well, ministers. Please seat yourselves."

The warriors took seat as Pharaoh Toui continued, "I asked you all here to review our military status and to better acquaint myself with the leadership. Will you have your deputies introduced, War Minister?"

The first officer stood, "I'm Sagazi, my liege, first deputy to War Minister Saabon, and liaison to all commanders."

Each officer stood and did likewise, taking time to explain conditions on the ground under their command. After which Pharaoh Toui offered breakfast and asked Saabon to remain for further discussions.

Morning sunbeams penetrated the hall's openings, giving warmth to the dingy air of contention.

"Your deputies reports were thorough, Minister. Accordingly, I'm assured peace resides in our outer territories."

"Most certainly, my Lord Pharaoh, deception is not tolerated among the ranks."

"Well-spoken Saabon, however you and I both know a woman Pharaoh is a radical change from our way of thinking, and our soldiers must accept change and stand accordingly."

Saabon stood attentive saying nothing.

"I take your silence as affirmation, Minister. Is Imani still stationed at Tunica?"

"She is, my liege. I ordered her to remain there indefinitely."

"Then relieve her and station her forces near Pharaoh's Mountain. She deserves a reward for her decisiveness during the Tunica attack."

Saabon nodded sharply replying, "As you wish my liege."

"Breakfast is served, Minister. Please join me." Saabon grunted and followed his Pharaoh.

Pharaoh's Army was operated by a chain of command that was comprised of ten deputies. The first deputy was a liaison to Saabon and commanded a communication relay system of 4,000 horsemen. The second deputy, in alliance with the six governor-priest militias, defended valley proper and command an additional 12,000 regulars. The third through eighth deputies were responsible for the territories south of the third cataract and each commanded 10,000 or more, depending on deployment priority. Saabon's ninth and tenth deputies, with a force of 30,000 combined, guarded the north and south Sahara trade routes. Promotion to higher rank was obtained by a majority vote from Saabon's staff or when Pharaoh reward a soldier for exemplary service. Even then, Saabon's staff had to vote on the promotion under the watchful eyes of Pharaoh; a clever strategy concocted out of the past to maintain the Pharaoh's leadership over the army.

A year later, drizzling rain welcomed Imani's military contingent; they tread past Pharaoh's Mountain enroute to their new headquarters. The small, well-stocked post near Pharaoh's Mountain was a sanctuary for soldiers returning from battle and housing Imani's forces, satisfying both Pharaoh's and Saabon's needs.

Pharaoh's regular army was unaware of a high-ranking woman within their ranks. The woman's command was instituted as an example of fairness but not yet acclimated into the army's way of thinking. With the Erastus Dynasty now being led by a woman, Saabon now had to acquaint his soldiers to the reality of change and stationed Imani near the seat of power accomplished the need.

Imani's command settled comfortably and she began to refit her embattled forces, requisitioning new armaments, chariots, and younger horse soldiers to replace retiring older ones.

Imani was tall, brown-skinned and well-proportioned. With a rhythmic gait, she strode into Pharaoh's gathering hall. She had nappy hair which draped to her shoulders and framed her oval-shaped face. Adorned with clear brown eyes, a smooth rounded nose, and clearly defined lips, Imani portrayed strong femininity. On this particular day, she was dressed in a light-green, knee length shirt which was tightly wrapped around her waist by a scabbard belt, toting a tied down blade; wide straps laced up her thick-soled sandals and guarded muscular calves.

She stopped, bowed to one knee, and greeted Pharaoh. The hall's gathering was festive with children in attended; all applauded Imani's appearance.

"We welcome you, Imani. Your courageous spirit made its presence here long before you arrived, and we applaud you."

Toui stood and began clapping; the congregation joined tumultuously. The children encircled Imani, singing songs of praise while others laid gifts at her feet. The Pharaoh placed a necklace with a hanging scarab around Imani's neck as Imani bowed and gave thanks.

"We have prepared a special feast. Will you join Minister Saabon and I?" asked Pharaoh Toui.

"With pleasure, however I humbly request my captain, Jabari accompany me, Lord Pharaoh."

"We are happy for him as well, war woman," replied the Pharaoh, rising from her seat as all followed her toward the eating chamber.

The table was set in the valley of the River Nile with Pharaoh Toui at the head and war minister Saabon at the foot. Imani and Captain Jabari were seated on the right while Deserae and Deserate were seated on the left.

The feast offered a spread of baked and roasted meats, cooked and fresh vegetables, a variety of fruits, and freshly baked bread on the side.

Pharaoh Toui, stood, and with goblet in hand pronounced, "I salute you all. Will the captain in our midst stand and introduce himself?"

Imani's captain, a tall, skinny man stood and said, "I am Captain Jabari, commander of Imani's chariot offensive;" he bowed and sat. The blessing said, and all began eating.

When supper was finished and the table was cleared, Pharaoh Toui conversed with the group.

"During my travel, I noticed women are unrepresented in most of the dynasty's leadership gatherings. Once removed from men's pallets, we become invisible."

Captain Jabari put a hand to his mouth stifling a giggle.

"You have something to add, Captain?" asked the Pharaoh.

"No," Jabari replied, shaking his head, "Your bluntness of words tickled me. I apologize for the interruption."

"Its fine captain, laughter is good for the soul, just as women being allowed to fulfill their dreams is good for the soul."

The Pharaoh paused, allowing her analogy to penetrate.

"Our dynasty must utilize all it talents for advance, as well as survival; gender notwithstanding. For your outstanding service, Imani, I offer you a promotion. The war minister and I shall discuss the details and notify you later. You and your captain are dismissed."

Imani and her captain stood, bowed, and gave thanks. Deserae and Deserate escorted them from the eating chamber.

"Imani is an impressive woman. What is her duty?"

"She is under command of my second deputy, my liege. Her force moves wherever needed to ward off criminal bands and other malcontents. They are just one of four groups deployed throughout the valley."

"She appears to be a person of very few words," Toui noted.

"True, Lord Pharaoh. Imani does not waste speech, however I'm told she and that skinny captain are tenacious in battle. I witnessed her aggressive nature at Siwa. The morning after our victory, I noticed her war chariots had silently crept within fighting range, anxious to battle."

"Impressive indeed," exclaimed Toui, "I want her promoted to the eleventh member of your staff, Minister. How soon can you arrange a vote?"

Saabon stuttered, "Lord Pharaoh, a promotion that high is fraught with many uncertainties, and because your army is mannish by nature, it responds best when such changes are gradual."

Toui bristled a little and said sharply, "Minister Saabon, perhaps you have noticed that men have less balance without nearness of women. So do my "mannish" army a favor and prepare a vote forty days from now. Are there any more questions?"

"Not at this time, my liege," Saabon answered tersely.

"Then I shall see you the morning of the fortieth day."

Saabon bowed and headed toward an exit; at the same time, Deserae and Deserate returned to the eating chamber.

Without looking up from her seat, Toui raised her voice and said, "Don't you two nymphs need to attend those men stashed away in your quarters?"

The aides hurriedly went. Saabon heard the exchange of words while leaving and grinned.

CHAPTER #10
DRUMBEAT OF WAR

Toui the First had her way; war woman Imani was promoted to Saabon's eleventh deputy and commandant of Pharaoh's northern army. She was assigned to defend the north from seafaring invaders.

Eager to prove worth, Imani hurriedly deploy bastions along the Mediterranean's southern coast, finishing in less than 2 years. When Imani reported to army headquarters, war minister Saabon refused her report and suggested it might be best for her to report directly to Pharaoh's Mountain. However Imani, a staunch, military-schooled officer, recognized Saabon's refusal as breach of military protocol and told him so.

"I'm unaware of any directive allowing me to bypass the chain of command, Minister. I am a battle-hardened soldier and beyond the pawns of politics. War is my forte, and I will not approach Pharaoh uninvited. With your permission, I shall now return to my headquarters." Imani turned and started toward her chariot.

"Hold, Deputy," Saabon called, "I shall review your report."

Imani boarded her chariot, handed Saabon the tablet, and ordered her driver to "move this chariot soldier I have duties elsewhere."

Watching the chariot speed away Saabon pointed saying, "I pity the fool that falls in love with her. Excusing that woman going yonder, Guard, summon all staff members here on the sixtieth day."

Promoting Imani to Saabon's command forced him to shuffle proud men about who were unwilling to relinquish power. The unexpected change increased grumbling. The winds of change gusted over the Nile valley, permeated with scents of women; Saabon believed it threatened the dynasty's way of life. For reasons of his own, he must now stymie the change or eliminate cause, Saabon choose latter.

Sixty days later, Saabon's deputies arrived, gathered in chamber waiting to hear his plan. Deputy Imani was not in attendance.

"The 'fork in the road' prediction leveled on Erastus the Tenth has arrived," Saabon told deputies.

"And it threatens a way of life that must be maintained. It is your duty to remove the woman from atop Pharaoh's Mountain and here shall be the base of operation. Study the situation; I shall devise a plan and issue orders later. That's all for now; dismissed."

Meanwhile back at Pharaoh's Mountain, Toui the First sensed Saabon's doubt, that her rise to power was entering new phase. She summoned her captain of the guard, a shadowy fellow who controlled the dynasty's clandestine activity.

The captain entered and bowed greetings, "And how may I serve you, Lord Pharaoh? He asked."

"I want information, Captain. There is grumbling within my army, and I need to know its severity. How soon can you submit a report?"

"I can respond within sixty days, my liege."

"Make haste then, Captain."

The soldier started to leave when Pharaoh called out, "Captain, no one here knows your name. Why is that?"

"There are a number of us stationed here and about, my liege, and we are honor-bound to serve you in secrecy."

"Very well, Captain. You're dismissed."

"Captain Nameless" obtained the information needed and reported back to Pharaoh's Mountain in less than the sixty days.

It read:

> Most commanders vow loyalty to Saabon, except the first, ninth, and tenth deputies, who support you, Lord Pharaoh. The loyal deputies guard Sahara's vital trade routes, and their loyalty to Pharaoh's Mountain is steadfast; old school veterans who would never entertain thoughts of rebellion. Reserve defenders of the Nile valley proper, as well as their junior officers, also stand solidly behind you, my liege. Discussions are ongoing and Saabon has not exposed his exact plan.

Toui the First thanked the captain, walked onto a balcony, and watched as night cloaked the Valley.

Deputy Imani was summoned to Pharaoh's Mountain two days later. The Pharaoh ordered her there for war talk. Imani took a seat as aides offered refreshments.

"I'm told you have experimented with Elephant warfare," Toui began. "Tell me what you have learned."

"We worked with ten elephant for two years, my liege. When used properly, they are very effective in battle, however command big appetites."

"Can charging elephants repulse masses of charging war chariots?"

"Most certainly, my liege. The only question regarding that is tactics and strategy."

"How much time is needed to train such a force, and is there a place where it can be done in secret?" asked Toui.

"Two or more years should be ample, my Pharaoh. Captain Jabari will find such a place; animals are fond of him."

"Then let it be done, but it is most important the undertaking be kept secret."

"I understand, my liege. Any soldier entrusted with such a mission shall not have reason to leave the training site, and we shall maintain an entertaining atmosphere for any prying eyes."

"Very well. There is another matter of utmost importance, Imani. Time and events have heaped enormous tasks upon me, and I must burden you with a shared sentence to duty."

"I'm not oblivious to the womanly winds of change, my liege, and any trust you place in me can only serve my needs. Your leadership position here invites destiny, and I welcome it," Imani said reverently.

"Your understanding is without equal, Imani. You are dismissed."

Back at headquarters, Imani ordered one hundred disguised soldiers, led by captain Jabari, northeast to hamlet Elephantine, so named for the elephant breeding ground. He and operatives were to herd the elephants to a secure location and begin military training.

All the while, talk of rebellion forced Pharaoh Toui's loyalists to gather at respective headquarters to plan movement. Toui the First was so pleased there was no rebellion from the guardian of essential trade routes that she dispatched Captain Nameless to the western border area to offer gratitude. The commanders received her envoy honorably.

Captain Nameless then returned to Pharaoh's Mountain and reported all was well on the western front. Pharaoh Toui then dispatched her trotting captain to Province Four to ascertain military significance of Kumen's barge fleet. The captain, along with twenty operatives, arrived disguised as a trader from Aswan, and infiltrated Kuman's bartering centers, quickly. They spread word that they had weapons for trade, and the amount offered was much more than the governor needed for defense. Kumen's acceptance indicated rebellious intent.

"I need three barges with crew for transport," the captain encouraged, after they struck a deal.

The governor agreed and allowed the operatives to board at port Dendara. However unbeknownst to Kumen, Captain Nameless' men had orders to seize control at first opportunity then hold barge crews until further orders. Captain Nameless then made haste back to Pharaoh's Mountain with information he thought detrimental to Pharaoh Toui's rule.

"Lord Pharaoh your suspicion was correct. Governor Kumen is tilted wrong," Captain Nameless reported as he and Pharaoh strolled about palace grounds.

"I'm not surprised, as he showed little respect during my visit. Now tell me something I don't know."

"Kumen's daughter,, named Najeebah is Saabon's Mama; and Saabon's father is none other than Erastus the Ninth. Najeebah was not Pharaoh's chosen woman therefore her son was denied the rights of first born.

"Saabon is Erastus the Tenth's half-brother and uncle to your son, Lord Pharaoh. His quick rise to war minister was appeasement."

Toui the First stopped and faced her captain saying, "Family affairs are most intense, but I shall not allow the Erastus Dynasty to shatter. Issue summons to loyalists, including governor priests, have them here forty days from now, return now to Province Four, at the proper time you shall command Kumen's 4,000 regulars. If and when that fool returns from this Mountain, place him under arrest."

Toui the First again summoned War Minister Saabon. When entering the gathering hall, she found Saabon's second-in-command standing, instead.

"Has calamities befell my war minister, Deputy?" asked Pharaoh.

"No, Lord Pharaoh," the deputy, Othon, answered.

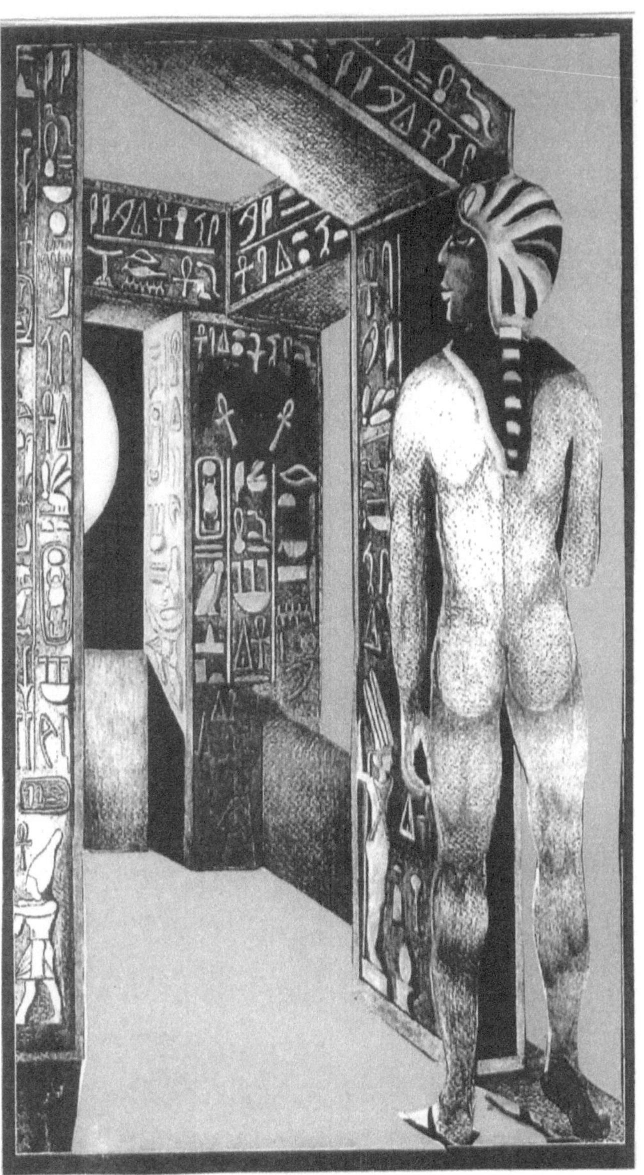

"Is everything in proper order at army headquarters, Deputy?"

"It is Lord Pharaoh," Othon again said, keeping his answers short.

"Then return to your duties. I, Pharaoh, am not amused by uninvited guests!"

Deputy Othon departed the gathering hall with quickness!

"Aide," said Pharaoh Toui, "fetch Ed-tutn-Nut and have him in my chamber at sundown. Saabon has trample my last nerve, and I am in need of a spanking."

CHAPTER #11
CHARIOTS OF WAR

During Saabon's lifetime, sagacious demeanor consistently portrayed the posture of leadership. His ancestor's spirit kept him regal against complacency. It had been difficult for him to stand aside, believing another claimed his birthright.

His father passed into the tomb, and the strongest opposition to his rise to power went with him. He now believed the winds of change gusting over the Nile Valley finally offered him opportunity.

Saabon dispatched envoys to each governor-priest, explaining his family lineage and strongly soliciting support. All flatly refused except Governor Kumen of Province Four. Those rejections sealed Saabon's rebellious plans. He had already ordered Deputy Othon to face Pharaoh in his stead, a condescending act which forced him to abandon army headquarters, and organized loyalists which were stationed south.

Saabon hastily assembled a military caravan and departed for *Abu Simbel,* headquarters of his third-ranking deputy. It was a station quite suitable for his plan, which was to muster 25,000 soldiers and march them north into a threatening position. He wanted to send a clear message to Pharaoh Toui the First that she must relinquish power and allow him his birthright.

Meanwhile, back at Pharaoh's Mountain, Toui the First held court. Dust from Saabon's caravan had not yet settled before she removed Deputy Othon, confined him to house arrest, and asked

Stephen Fetchum, a retired high-ranking deputy, to take charge.

Pharaoh addressed the court, "We are witnessing division within my army, marshaling toward a military takeover; and I shall meet the challenge head-on.

"Minister Saabon has abandoned army headquarters and gone south to organize his fellow conspirators. However, my advisors tell me it will take him three or more years of preparation before he can attack."

The gathering became raucous, voicing disbelief.

"I've appointed Stephen Fetchum as interim war minister. From here on out, we will be working vigorously to stop Saabon which will require selfless effort from all. Stephen Fetchum, you may speak."

A six foot tall, thin man with a high pitched voice stood and addressed the court, "Lord Pharaoh, honored ministers, I'm charged with vanquishing all the Nile Valley's enemies, whoever and wherever I find them. I have known Saabon all of his life; and because of his heritage, he believe none under God's sun can deny him a seat of power. Of course, he is wrong; Saabon will battle thinking he is right. A worthy opponent possessing unworthy incentives, whom I shall defeat."

Stephen Fetchum reclaimed his seat.

"From this day forward we must quicken performances," added Pharaoh Toui, "ensuring our army is well equipped and well fed.

"Secondly, the people of the River Nile must not lack necessities. Stores must be kept at capacity.

Excuses from anyone shall be wasted talk. The minister of procurements will tell you what is needed. Get busy, this meeting is adjourned."

Stephen Fetchum recognized immediately the threat posed by Kumen's barges fleet. While Kumen visited Pharaoh's Mountain, war minister Fetchum mustered a sizable force and rushed to Province Four. With Captain Nameless' help, they secured Kumen's headquarters and the war minister returned to Pharaoh's Mountain in time for the staff meeting. A full gathering of officials awaited him.

In the gathering hall's center aisle, five priests sat with Kumen and his staff.. High ranking military deputies occupied the right of aisle, and department heads were seated left aisle.

Pharaoh Toui entered and all stood as she seated herself. Scribes opened their tablets as she began to speak, "Will the keeper of the dynasty's edicts rise and denounce Saabon's rebellion?"

The five priests stood and one spoke, "As we have said before, Lord Pharaoh, none other than you has a claim to your throne. The dynasty's edicts are unequivocal on this matter; Erastus the Ninth did not recognize Najeebah's son as first-born." The priests bowed and took seat.

"Is there anyone within the sound of my voice that disagrees?" asked Pharaoh.

Kumen and his staff stood, bowed, and began to leave. Guards at the exits crossed their spears threateningly. Kumen's group stopped. Toui's hand gestured toward the guards; and they stepped aside, allowing passage.

Upon leaving Pharaoh's Mountain, Kumon felt uneasy. His uncontested exit made him suspicious, and instead of returning to his headquarters he and his band guided their chariots toward port Dendara, the village where Kumen's barges fleet moored. After arriving, they secluded themselves to ponder their next move.

At the same time, back in Province Four, Captain Nameless learned his men were unsuccessful in overpowering Kumen's sailors. Somehow barge crews discovered the plot, subdued the operatives, and set them adrift. Now Captain Nameless was forced to go to Dendara and secure Kumen's barges before they set sail.

The fast moving old man was one step ahead, however. Informed of the failed plot, he rallied his sailors and sailed south with forty barges. When Captain Nameless arrived at Dendara, he discovered the port leader had also departed with the fleet.

The captain established control and then sent a report of the situation to Pharaoh Toui. She messaged him back to hold position until further orders.

The time was approaching three years since Pharaoh's army split, and Saabon's command of 25,000 remained far south. Scouts reported that Saabon's army was well fed and well equipped but not yet on the move. Kumen's barge fleet infused a formidable addition to Saabon's forces, and in appreciation Saabon promoted him to captain. For the past three years, barges ferried supplies from territories further south. Saabon's army was ready to move, yet they waited, constantly sharpening their shiny blades.

Events were festive back at Pharaoh's Mountain. Little Erastus celebrated his tenth birthday. The milestone concluded his in-house tutoring; and he was now to attend secondary school until rites of passage. After rites of passage, boy Erastus would enter Pharaoh's private school of thought where teachers would transform his thinking into the mindset of a Pharaoh. The many hours of schooling kept the boy apart from his mama, a well-deserved separation to say the least. Toui the First didn't have time for mothering as most of her waking hours were spent preparing for war.

Meanwhile, Pharaoh's loyalists were on the move. Deputy Tutut-um, guardian of the dynasty's southwestern trade routes, moved 12,000 of his 15,000 men east to Fayum Oasis, a large watering hole that lay south of its twenty mile-long namesake, Fayum Pass. Both were in direct line toward Pharaoh's Mountain and had been used for centuries by southern invaders attempting conquer.

Tutut-um ordered to defend both; because Saabon's success depended on capturing the oasis first; and then he must maneuver the centuries old battleground toward Fayum Pass. Now if that specious battleground could talk, it would first heave the blood of countless fell warriors, and had their crimson bled been indelible, blackened ground would surround!

The tides had changed in the valley of the River Nile. Saabon, once arch-defender, would soon invade. The first major attack was against deputy

Tutut-um. A fighting force prepared to launch 1,000 war chariots from Oasis Fayum's southern perimeter with 4,000 archers holding at rear. Further back, 3,000 spears and shields were positioned in such a manner to discourage attack from different directions. The rest of the force were to remain as barriers inside Fayum Pass as a last stand effort. With the defense set, Tutut-um sent word to war minister Fetchum.

It read, "if and when Saabon enters Fayum Pass, he will leave blood and pride at Oasis Fayum."

Tutut-um's grossly outnumbered forces shined and sharpened their keen blades then settled down to rest.

Meanwhile, war minister Stephen Fetchum began executing his attack. He ordered 6,000 regulars to muster on him at Province Four. Then he relieved Captain Nameless and directed him back to Pharaoh's Mountain.

Deputy Tuskin, guardian of the dynasty's northern trade routes, was ordered to march south and secure both the Farafra and Dakla Oasis enroute to join muster.

Tuskin reported to Province Four with 5,000 men in tow. The message Deputy Imani received instructed her to keep a watchful eye against war profiteers; and with her remaining forces, set a defense north of Pharaoh's Mountain. When she completed the task, Imani waited at her headquarters, ready with 5,000 soldiers.

War minister Fetchum, alerted the people of Province Four to the imminence of war. After which he with deputy Tuskin forces abandoned the province and began his march toward Fayum's Pass.

In the past, when southern invaders tried to advance on Pharaoh's Mountain, they faced the bulk of Pharaoh's Army at north exit Fayum Pass. Any enemy with hope of success had to avoid being jammed inside. It was war minister Saabon who improved the jamming defense, and he would most certainly avoid trappings of his own schemes.

Saabon never lost a battle at Fayum Pass. Before invaders would exit, his jamming defense forced them to turn about in very little space causing mass confusion; the invaders would then practically defeat themselves. War minister Stephen Fetchum was confident and aware of Saabon's strategies, and watched with glee as his forces rallied for defense. Bright sunshine flashed off thousands of sky-pointed spears, menacing even more the tranquility of peace during lull before war.

Another thirty days passed, and Saabon army had not moved. Pharaoh Toui called her commanders to council.

"Almost four years has passed, deputies. Why is Saabon's army not advancing?"

"We dictate his strategy, my Pharaoh," spoke Stephen Fetchum. "Saabon expected a challenge earlier, and when it did not occur he realized your army was not prepared. Now he is ready to fight but so are we. Saabon must take the offensive, which burden his army with many problems; we are defensive and can wait.

"Saabon's army will not move north until he is certain your army will not move south, my liege. I think he expects you to be impatient."

A messenger entered the gathering hall and addressed Pharaoh Toui, "Deputy Imani requests an audience at your earliest convenience, my Pharaoh."

"Very well, have her in the palace at sunrise, tomorrow. And war minister...I want you here as well. We are adjourned."

That next day, Deputy Imani reported Captain Jabari was ready to deploy 100 military-trained elephants. Although training was not yet complete, handlers had enough control to be effective.

"Just how effective are they?" asked the Pharaoh.

"We are able to stampede the herd at will and force them to hold a reasonably straight line. Although, once stampeding, they become expendable and run until exhausted, trampling everything within their path; we cannot retrieve them during battle, my liege."

"Does Saabon know about these trained elephants?" asked Stephen Fetchum.

"I didn't tell him. Did you?" Toui answered, gesturing toward Imani.

Imani shook her head negatively and said nothing.

"Where are these elephants, and how soon can they arrive at Fayum Pass?" Toui asked.

"We anticipated your need," Imani answered. "My captain is twenty days away and can move at night if so ordered."

"It shall be a pleasure to meet this ingenious captain of yours, Imani," Stephen Fetchum said. "With your permission, my liege, I request Jabari's elephant brigade start toward Fayum Pass as soon as possible."

"Very well, it is so ordered. Minister Fetchum, how much time is needed to move my army through Fayum Pass?"

"No more than twenty days once we arrive at the opening, Lord Pharaoh, but–"

"Very well, Minister," Pharaoh interrupted. "You both are dismissed. Aide, send in a guard captain."

The captain arrived promptly.

"Captain, I can't get Kumen and his barge fleet out of my mind. How many soldiers can one barge float?"

"We estimate up to fifty, Lord Pharaoh."

"Then do what is needed to report the fleet movement. I know it shall take time but I will sleep better knowing the whereabouts of that old man."

CHAPTER # 12
FOUL PLAY EXPOSED

Deserae and Deserate had requested leave of absence. Attending Pharaoh's beckon call during war preparation had caused weariness.

"I could use some recluse, myself," Toui acknowledged. "Take as much time as you need."

Back at recluse, Minister Isaiah greeted the twins warmly, "Welcome home you two. I'm very happy to see you. Take time refresh yourselves. We must talk later."

Unbeknownst to Pharaoh, the aides did not return to the recluse for just rest and recuperation. Minister Isaiah had requested their presence and obliged not to burden Pharaoh un-necessarily.

That evening the twins sat, facing Isaiah.

"Your loyalty to people you care about has been unshakable the past eight years," Isaiah said, without looking up from a tablet he was studying.

Deserae and Deserate did not respond.

"The sudden death of Pharaoh has edged this valley to the brink of internal war, and I need details of what happened that only you can provide."

Isaiah looked up at the twins saying nothing more. Silence lingered, finally Deserae spoke.

"My sister and I know nothing more than what we told War Minister Saabon,"

"Very well. I asked you here for two reasons, your loyalty to Pharaoh Toui and secondly your closeness to woman Toui.

"My questions shall not force you to violate either, however the deadly consequences facing our homeland require us all to share blame. Denying guilt offers little solace and shall not stop the flow of blood, but if blood must flow, we must ensure the cause is just.

"There is a visitor here from Village Edfu who I want you to see, and I hope she will help you remember everything that happened that night."

In walked a tall, brown-skinned elderly woman with a distraught look upon her face. Deserae and Deserate stared at her wide-eyed and put their hands over their faces, bending their heads to their laps. The woman touched each lightly and departed.

"Lift your heads, twins," Isaiah said. "You came here for rest and recuperation, the recluse does not disappoint clients."

The aides sat attentive, they and Isaiah talked long into the night.

Twenty days later Desarae and Deserate returned to Pharaoh's Mountain. During supper, Pharaoh Toui praised their appearance.

"I see a recluse gleam in your eyes and a lively color to your skin. Minister Isaiah must have been particularly attendant to obtain such results in short order. Welcome back. Having you at my side pleases me immensely."

"The feeling is mutual, Lord Pharaoh," the twins said in unison.

"Tell me about Isaiah. Is he well?"

"Very well, my liege, and as dictatorial as ever. He sends his greeting."

"I haven't spoken with him since his encounter with Saabon. Has the suspicion of foul play caused much distress?"

"On the contrary, my liege, Isaiah has been strengthened by what he called the white-washing of Recluse of Min. He is working extremely hard to divert any guilt pointing towards his beloved station," Deserate answered.

Deserae joined in, "Isaiah has a finished report for your eyes only, my liege. He didn't want to burden you unnecessarily during these trying times so he confided us to remain silent. Now that war is imminent, I'm sure the minister shall visit Pharaoh's Mountain most urgently."

"Very well, take time and get reacquainted. My demands remain most vigorous during the drumbeat of war," Toui said, finishing her meal.

The following morning, Minister Isaiah arrived and requested an audience. Pharaoh Toui invited him to breakfast. They talked, laughed together, and rehashed old times.

"Tell me about your investigation. What is that all about?" Toui asked.

Isaiah handed Pharaoh a tablet.

"You'll find everything I've learned here in writing. I hope the information offers peace of mind and aids you in the decisions you must make."

"We shall examine your work carefully, Minister, and act accordingly."

I know you must leave tomorrow, however accept a Pharaoh's hospitality tonight."

"With utmost pleasure, Lord Pharaoh," Isaiah replied.

At Saabon's southern command, the battle plan was finalized. Saabon shall march north with an army of 4,000 war chariots, 4,000 horse soldiers with spears, 6,000 archers, and 10,000 foot soldiers with spear and shield, Another 2,000 support personnel with water-bearing camels followed at close order. Saabon divide his forces into three divisions. The first division, commanded by deputy Fleeta, marched north along the banks of the River Nile. The second division with him commanding moved parallel to Fleeta's forces ten miles inland. Further inland, the third division, with Deputy Tuhu in charge, marched likewise.

His command staff assembled Saabon spoke, "Deputies, we start north in four days. Forward way stations are set ten days apart, so hold your direction straight north as long as possible. In thirty days all divisions shall converge on Oasis Kharga, the first prolonged stop. With combined forces, we shall march toward Oasis Fayum.

"Captain Kumen's barge fleet has already sailed with 1,600 men, and ordered to attack Pharaoh's Mountain northern perimeter as we approach from the south. If all goes as planned, we shall gaze on Oasis Fayum within sixty days. A word of caution however, before drinking cooling water of Oasis Fayum, we will face deputy Tutut-um's defense. The man is a battlefield strategist' without reservations his 12,000 soldiers will cast blind eyes on our superior strength. Deputy Tuttut-um will fight until the last man standing."

Back at Pharaoh's Mountain, war reports were arriving daily. Kumen's barge fleet departed Abu-Simbel, destination still unknown. Saabon's army is marching north to arrive at Oasis Fayum within sixty days.

A captain entered and approached the Pharaoh, "Two of Saabon's messengers are outside awaiting audience," he said.

"Very well, escort them to me."

Guards brought in the two, forcing them to kneel.

"What is so important that you must interrupt your Pharaoh?"

"We are under command of Saabon. He–"

"Shut up! snapped Pharaoh. "You talk too much. I know what he wants. Now get off your knees and tell him he'll have my answer in due time."

The messengers departed the palace in full sprint, going quickly out of sight.

An aide silently approached, "My Pharaoh," speaking in whisper, "that mysterious woman from Village Edfu requests an audience."

"Very well, offer her a Pharaoh's hospitality. I shall meet with her at midday tomorrow. Have my aides resumed duties?"

"Not yet, my liege. They asked that I serve for two more days."

"Very well, now please leave me."

The same elderly woman that had previously visited the twins at the recluse entered Pharaoh's chamber the following day and conversed in private. Finally, the woman from Edfu emerged and instructed the aides not to disturb the sleeping Pharaoh; she then boarded a chariot and sped away.

Toui the First found herself at Village Edfu, a small settlement lying a few miles east of Pharaoh's Mountain. Adjacent to the village was a limestone plateau that housed sculptured Nuba trials.

A colonnade with rows of white columns led inside; the aesthetics had been unchanged for centuries. Every inch inside was rumored to portray colorful renderings of the dynasty's exploits. During past centuries, only caretakers with severed tongues were allowed entrance, with the exception of a Pharaoh preparing for war.

Toui the First arrived at Edfu and offered respect to the Village Mak, who counseled her for a short time and then walked with her toward the shrine's entrance. The Mak retreated toward the plateau's opening, directing Toui to proceed further. Darkness greeted Toui's first step then sunbeams from the skylights lit the rest of the way. Far ahead at the end of the path, sitting upright with eyes closed, was the oldest man she had ever seen. Sunrays illuminated his face, rendering definition of age. Covered from shoulder to foot in a purple smock, the old man did not acknowledge her presence.

"I, Pharaoh Toui the First, am here," she spoke softly, as instructed.

The Methuselah opened his eyes and began to speak. Pharaoh Toui stood attentive while a servant stood nearby, waiting to offer a glossy, scripted stone as a gift to the visiting Monarch. After a short while the Woman Pharaoh emerged into daylight.

At Pharaoh's Mountain, report of Kumen's movement showed his barge fleet north of Aswan, but his exact destination was still unknown. The former governor of Province Four had long harbored ill feeling toward Erastus' leadership. The bad-blood boiled years ago when Erastus the Ninth coveted Kumen's daughter, Najeebah. The sly Kumen had known Erastus the Ninth was a womanizer who did not follow the strict dictates inscribed in the dynasty's edicts. Being an opportunist and desiring recognition from the dynasty's higher-ups, Kumen maneuvered his unsuspecting daughter onto Pharaoh's pallet; and when she was with child, secretly petitioned the Pharaoh to anoint her as the chosen woman. Erastus the Ninth flatly refused and offered compensation: Najeebah' son, Saabon, was allowed to attend Pharaoh's private schools of thoughts but without recognition as first born.

Kumen hated the appeasement, but realized hate would not protect him against conflict with Erastus the Ninth, so he accepted the arrangement but with enviousness intent. The goal was clear: the old man would attempt to militarily remove anyone who occupied the throne atop Pharaoh's Mountain, other than his grandson.

Kumen's barge fleet arrived far north and moored in a cove across the Nile from Village Meidum. He called his boatswains to gather.

"Our destination is that settlement you see over the river," he said, pointing toward a cluster of dwelling. "We shall seize the place under guise of protection and use it as a base to launch attacks against the enemy. Our commander shall be in position to start his war in thirty days. At that time, we shall move on the enemy in force.

"Return to your crafts; there is no need for further secrecy. We will cross the River Nile at daybreak."

While Saabon's army was treading slowly toward Oasis Kharga, he was having second thoughts about unleashing his grandfather against Pharaoh's Mountain. Saabon suddenly realize Kumen's hatred toward the Erastus Dynasty made the selection a bad choice, and dispatched three messengers to Meidum, hoping one would get to Kumen in time.

One messenger did as much, to his demise. After hearing Saabon's instructions to hold onto the Nile's eastern shore, Kumen threw the messenger overboard then proceeded to Meidum. After securing Medium and conscripting all its able-bodied men, Kumen convinced the populace that their sons were in service to Pharaoh's Army. Kumen's revenge was within his grasp, and he reveled at the thought of greeting his grandson atop Pharaoh's Mountain as *Pharaoh Saabon the First.*

Kumen mustered 3,000 recruits during his stay at Meidum, with little concern for their fighting ability. A show of force was all he thought they would need against the lightly defended northern perimeter of Pharaoh's Mountain. He also obtained ten chariots for his command staff and armed his raw recruits with mostly spears and shields.

Pharaoh's Mountain stood southwest from Meidum across terrain directly in line with Pharaoh's old hunting ground, a spacious hardpan bordered by forested hills on one side and high limestone plateaus on the other; it was well suited for Kumen's intentions. Kumen hunted the area in his youth and would now use it for trappings of war.

At Pharaoh's Mountain, Toui was informed that Kumen arrived at Meidum.

"He has forces enough to threaten, my liege," a captain warned, "and it's only a twelve day march to your hunting grounds."

"Very well. That old man is determined, and today I shall plan his future. Dispatch a messenger to War Minister Stephen Fetchum and order him to prepare the army to move through Fayum pass."

The captain appeared stunned by the request.

"Is something wrong, Captain?" the Pharaoh asked.

"I'm confused, my Lord Pharaoh–"

"No worries, most dedicated one," Toui interrupted, "this change is my burden and you shall be at my side at every encounter. At this moment, I need fresh air; have my chariot brought about."

The chariot arrived promptly. Toui boarded, took the reins, and coached her steeds down the treacherous mountainside. At the bottom she wacked the horses into a full trot in route toward Imani's headquarters.

At post headquarters, Pharaoh Toui stopped in front of a waiting Imani.

"My guard saw your chariot at a distance, my liege. Are there problems?"

Without dismounting and still holding tight reins, Toni replied, "Yes, Imani. Not only did I need a ride this morning, but Kumen's forces will arrive within sight of Pharaoh's Mountain sooner than expected. I want you to offer him a proper greeting."

Pharaoh's horses bucked. Imani stepped forward, grabbed the bits, and the animals calmed.

"My scout already reported Kumen's movement, my liege. He is on course to reach the hunting ground in about nine days, and after arrival I expect him to camp beyond the northern hills until nightfall. He will enter the hunting ground under cover of darkness. The open space shall expose his forces, and we shall advance accordingly."

"Very well, Imani. I shall join you in this battle."

Imani rubbed the horse's forehead, released them, and then nodded as Pharaoh Toui wheeled her chariot back toward Pharaoh's Mountain.

Back at the palace, the horses held steady as Pharaoh stepped from the chariot.

"Captain," she said, "you and I shall join Deputy Imani on the battlefield in nine days. Prepare three war chariots and decorate them in a manner befitting Pharaoh's army."

"With long awaited pleasure, my liege."

"Are the guardeing of dynasty's edicts still on palace grounds?" Tour asked.

"Yes, Lord Pharaoh," answered an aide, "The Priests are duty-bound to remain close at hand during time of war."

"Very well, have them in my chamber tomorrow at sundown."

Toui the First spent the following day playing with her son. They walked about the palace grounds while she explained to him aspects of life. She told him about unpleasant things such as war, and asked that he not be afraid.

"I'm not afraid, Mama," little Erastus told her.

Later that evening, five priests arrived, met in privacy with Pharaoh, and then departed.

As the priests were leaving, Toui summoned an aide and said, "Prepare a pallet next to mine; I want my son near me, tonight."

Just as Deputy Imani predicted, Kumen waited beyond the plains of the northern hills and, under cover of darkness, crept onto the hunting ground. At the same time, Imani deployed 1,000 soldiers into position on the hunting ground's southern end.

Heavy fog rolled in as the soldiers positioned forward. Imani was aware her adversary was without chariot offensive, so she lined fifty war chariots in front of five hundred spears and shields with three hundred archers standing at the rear. The battlefield positions would hold until they were within fighting range, then the chariots would spread right and left while the spear and shield soldiers knelt. Archers would then prepare to launch while Imani's ten-chariot command staff would positioned behind the attacking chariots.

The morning fog thickened, seemingly intent on hiding Imani's war footing. Pharaoh Toui's chariots arrived, each displaying highflying banners embroidered with Pharaoh's insignias front and center.

Imani removed her war bonnet and nodded greetings.

"Kumen's battle formation is beyond that fog bank, and there is no indication he is aware of our presence. We will end his adventure on your command, my liege."

"End it quickly, Imani; we have other battles to fight."

Replacing her war bonnet, Imani pointed her spear north, and the battle formation marched forward.

At the same time, Kumen's motley army was rolling straight toward Imani's war footing. Believing Pharaoh's Mountain defenders were preoccupied with Saabon's advance, Kumen was in high spirits and did not notice the horse's unusual fractious and nervousness – the only indication something was amiss!

The sun rose, the fog lifted, and Kumen stopped. What he saw in front of him numbed him. His front soldiers began to murmur.

"Hold the line!" Kumen shouted.

A soldier broke rank ran alongside Kumen's chariot shouting, "That's Pharaoh's army, yonder; not an enemy. We have been duped!"

Kumen drew his spear and chunked it at the soldier, glancing his leg. The soldier fell and lay motionless.

"Forward," Kumen shouted! His soldiers *did not stir!*

Now within fighting range, Imani's war chariots began splitting left and right as the spear and shield soldiers knelt in front of archers with cocked bows. Command chariots followed, moving the attack chariots.

Captain Nameless dismounted Pharaoh's chariot and posed himself, ready to defend. Imani raised her launch flag but hesitated before dropping it.

"Lord Pharaoh," she shouted, "something is wrong here; the enemy is without a will to fight!"

"Then hold the launch, Imani!" Toui shouted back.

Captain Nameless tied a red cloth with Pharaoh's emblem to an arrow and shot it high into the air. The arrow landed behind Kumen's chariot.

A soldier retrieved the cloth and held it high shouting, "Pharaoh's army is yonder! Lay down your arms!"

Kumen turned and shot an arrow into the soldier, striking him dead. Others began discarding weapons as they retreated. Kumen kicked off his driver and headed east as chariots encircled the retreating soldiers, forcing them to surrender.

Imani approached Toui saying, "The rebels fleeing won't get far. I shall bring them as you wish, my liege."

"Bring them to me as *you* wish, Imani! shouted Pharaoh Toui, under the sounds of leather striking horseflesh. Toui's chariot wheeled and headed toward Pharaoh's Mountain.

"Seize those leaders and return with them to Pharaoh's Mountain," Imani ordered. "I will attend to Kumen myself."

The old man's escape was short lived. A chariot wheel broke, forcing him to stand alone. A defiant prey on the same ground he once roamed as predator.

Imani's horses pranced toward Kumen then stopped a short distance away. Imani dismounted with spear and shield and walked slowly towards him. With bow cocked, Kumen acted without repentance.

"Lay down your arms! You have a debt to pay!" Imani ordered.

Kumen unleashed an arrow; and Imani cocked her shield, forcing the dart to glance upward. Kumen quickly shot again. The arrow hit Imani's shield straight on and stuck.

"Your debt is on demand; put down your weapon, old man!" Imani again ordered.

Kumen fired a third arrow, again hitting Imani's shield. Without a hesitant step, the war woman launched her spear; it missed. Kumen stepped back as Imani drew her tied-down blade. The old man cocked his bow but with hesitation, shot; and that hesitant moment was his undoing. In that split second, Imani reared back and slung her heavy-handled blade. The blade flew end over end, point impaling Kumen below the neck. Clutching the blade with both hands, and as if defying gravity, Kumen fell slowly backward to the ground. Dead!

Back at the battle area, chariots held a line with prisoners in front. The war formation had performed an about face and waited for orders to return to post. Kumen's conscripts retrieved their weapons and headed home. Imani's chariot wheeled front and center, rolling south; Pharaoh's army followed.

CHAPTER #13
PHARAOH'S ARMY

Kumen's sarcophagus was placed inside Erastus the Third's palace.

"He is a member of the family," Pharaoh Toui acknowledged. "The recognition he so diabolically sought is finally his, albeit at the foot of this mountain. Let forgiveness reign."

"We shall prepare his internment befittingly, Lord Pharaoh," replied the minister of burial.

A messenger from Imani reported all threats from the north had been eliminated and remaining forces were enroute to Fayum Pass.

"Very well, are my chariots ready, Captain?"

"Yes, my liege. Ten chariots decorated as you instructed, and a most impressive display, indeed."

"Has the woman from Edfu arrived yet?" Pharaoh Toui asked.

"She has and is waiting your council on the south balcony, Lord Pharaoh."

"Very well all, we march at sunrise. Are you sure you're ready, Captain?"

"We are indeed, Lord Pharaoh; and shall hail thy lead with the rising sun."

"Then you are dismissed."

Pharaoh Toui departed toward the south balcony, applauded by all for her sobriety of mood and unwavering leadership.

"I greet you, Najeebah. I want to acknowledge your presence during these difficult times, especially your urge for me to visit your village.

The time spent was most enlightening. Now, how old is that Methuselah who resides there?"

"No one stays in that old place, Lord Pharaoh. It was sealed centuries ago and there is no entrance, however an old man is sometime seen ambling about. He is not known, although he and I, *and now you,* share each other's dreams."

"I'm well aware of our spiritual legacy, Najeebah. The trance you invited me into was replete with guidance. Offer my thanks to your mentor, Methuselah, at his next calling."

"I shall indeed, my Pharaoh; and your obedience to the ghost of Edfu has again ensured the dynasty's proper future," Najeebah said with a smile.

Pharaoh Toui stood and walked to the balcony's edge and peered toward the southern horizon.

"Najeebah, I must deny your request to join me in this battle. You have suffered enough, and I beseech you to return to your village and mend your wounds."

"I shall indeed, Lord Pharaoh. Thanks to you, I do so with an unburdened heart. My father, may he rest in peace, could not deny the demons within, and my son Saabon is driven by the spirit of Erastus the First. So I accept my pertinence and shall attend funerals if need be, but mourn only for the living."

Days later, Pharaoh's contingent joined forces at the northern exit of Fayum Pass.

"With your permission, Lord Pharaoh," spoke Stephen Fetchum, "I shall order Jabari's elephant brigade to defend here. The thoroughfare is most suitable for elephant warfare."

"That sounds like an excellent plan, Minister," agreed Toui. "Now let's have a look at the south end of this pass."

Twenty days later, Pharaoh's army arrived at Oasis Fayum, took drink, rested and joined the right flank with Tutut-um's forces. Imani's warriors joined the left formation; the massive war footing marched steadily south.

Meanwhile, Saabon's army had also moved within striking distance of the Oasis. Saabon was surprised to learn Pharaoh's army was marching south, so he hurriedly set his battle formation, positioning 3,000 horse and spear soldiers upfront, backed by 5,000 spear and shields. Next in line, 5,000 archers stood with 3,000 chariots at the rear in a wide formation. His remaining horses and spears were posted further at the rear.

The sun shone hot on that dusty hardpan as the two massive armies moved slowly toward each other. Suddenly! Saabon waved his halt flag. Off in the distance he saw Pharaoh's ten chariots over a rise, with high flying flags blowing gallantly. Saabon watched as Pharaoh's army came wave after wave. They were an exact duplicate of his war formation and stretching just as wide.

Pharaoh's army stopped within fighting range. A horse soldier broke rank, galloping midway between the two, and chucked a spear into the ground. The age-old sanctifying gesture that disallowed blood spilled while talking. The grounded spear also allowed time for a Pharaoh to move from harm's way if negotiation failed.

Saabon dismounted, removed weapons and war bonnet, then approach the embedded spear. Woman Toui, along with Deserae and Deserate who were carrying long-stemmed shading palms, did likewise. Saabon and woman Toui stood face-to-face on the wide, open battlefield without sanctuary; armies poised for battle. The sounds of clanking weapons and neighing horses were the only disturbance

Saabon's voice broke the silence, "You are forcing me to spill blood of Amarna, Woman!" he shouted.

"I force you to do nothing, Saabon!" Toui shouted back. "Your idolater grandfather who is responsible for this violence is dead. He lay in-state at the foot of Pharaoh's Mountain, victimized by an encounter with war woman Imani on the battlefield. Your mother is aware of these happenings and has returned to her home to find peace.

"Kumen was at Recluse of Min the night of Erastus the Tenth's death. He tampered with Pharaoh's drink, using Deserae and Deserate as unwitting accomplices."

"Your words are disheartening, Woman, but also have the tone of truth. Nevertheless, I demand you relinquish power and allow me my birthright," Saabon growled.

"You have no demands, Saabon! At your urging, I gave birth to Erastus the Eleventh. Now throw down your arms!"

Saabon bristled! "Remove that spear from the ground, Woman!" he shouted. "It blocks my path to Pharaoh's Mountain!

Saabon turned and started toward his chariot as Toui beckoned toward hers.

Before Saabon got to his chariot, a child's voice rang out, "Hold Saabon and face Pharaoh!"

Saabon stopped and hesitated, before slowly turning his head.

"I, Pharaoh, command you," the voice sounded. "Lay down your arms!"

Saabon turned and there stood four feet tall Erastus the Eleventh, boy Pharaoh. A crown encrusted with gold inlaid vulture and cobra insignias lay on his head; his small hands clutched the whip and scepter symbols of dominion. A wrap-around skirt with matching laced-up sandals completed boy Pharaoh's dress, and Saabon knew instantly his appearance could not be without anointment by the guardians of the dynasty's edicts.

"Throw down these weapons, uncle!" boy Pharaoh again ordered. "There shall be no war here, this day."

Saabon stepped back, stood at attention, and nodded his head saying, "Your wishes shall forever command me, oh mighty Pharaoh."

Sunset crept over that centuries-old battleground, silhouetting long shadows from the withdrawing armies. But most ominous of all, the horse soldiers charged with removing the sanctifying spear *did not stir!*

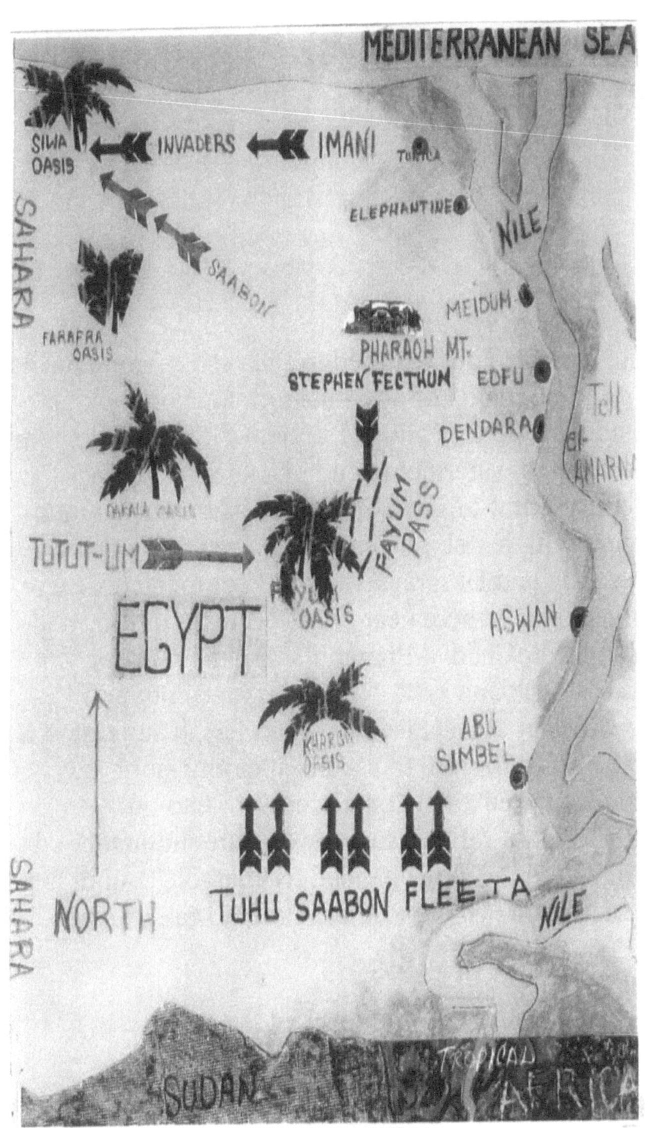

MEDITERRANEAN SEA
SAHARA
SILWA OASIS
INVADERS
IMANI
TUFITA
ELEPHANTINE
NILE
SAABON
MEIDUM
FARAFRA OASIS
PHARAOH MT.
STEPHEN FECTHUM
EDFU
DENDARA
Tell el-AMARNA
DAKALA OASIS
FAYUM PASS
TUTUT-LIM
FAYUM OASIS
EGYPT
ASWAN
KHARON OASIS
ABU SIMBEL
SAHARA
NORTH
TUHU SAABON FLEETA
NILE
SUDAN
TROPICAL AFRICA

EPILOGUE

The woman Toui returned to Pharaoh's Mountain as a minding mama of boy Pharaoh. Saabon took up residence there as advisor to both. Stephen Fecthum returned to watermelon and blackberry tending. Deputy Tutut-um was appointed war minister, and Imani with her skinny captain retired to Tunica. Deserate and Deserae and their kept men chose a village somewhere near "The Recluse of Min." Ed-tut-nut remained at Pharaoh's mountain under Toui's beck and call.. Nnowwo was appointed headmaster at Recluse and when Isaiah suggested it was alright for him to use his standing stool, it almost started a fist-fight, Nnowwo had no intentions of relinquishing his newfound manhood. The inscripted stone handed to Pharaoh Toui in her dream read: "Uncle Remos, eternal Mak of Nuba."

About the author

Henry Mpagazi

Aka Henry Howard

Born in the delta near Greenwood Mississippi

March 26 1934

Raised Peoria Illinois

Soldier, Airman, bpp member and San Francisco

cable car gripman

Passionate pre-history buff

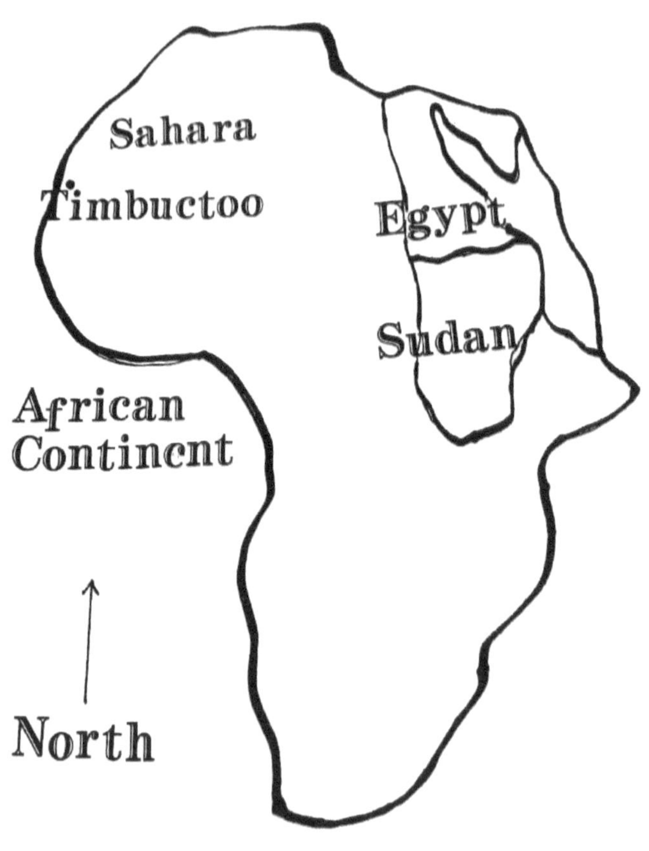

Sahara
Timbuctoo
Egypt
Sudan
African
Continent
North

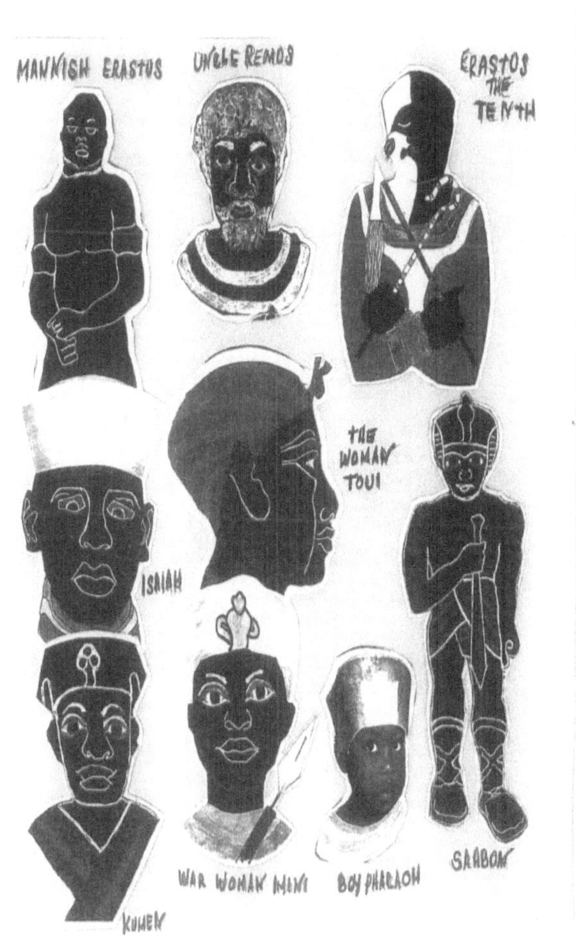

MANNISH ERASTUS
UNCLE REMOS
ERASTOS THE TENTH
THE WOMAN TOUI
ISAIAH
WAR WOMAN MINI
BOY PHARAOH
GAABON
KUMEN

#003

#005

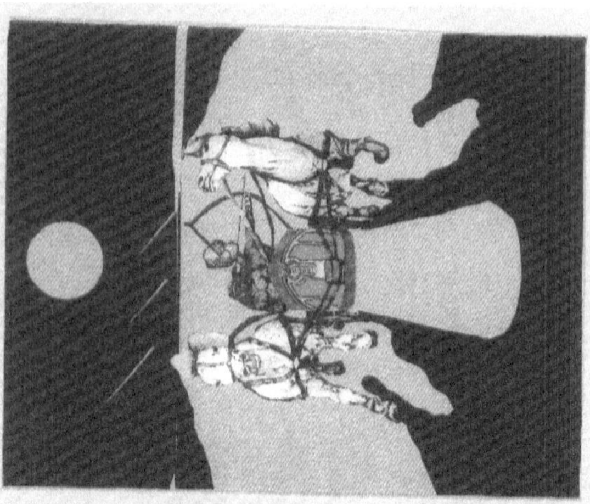

#006

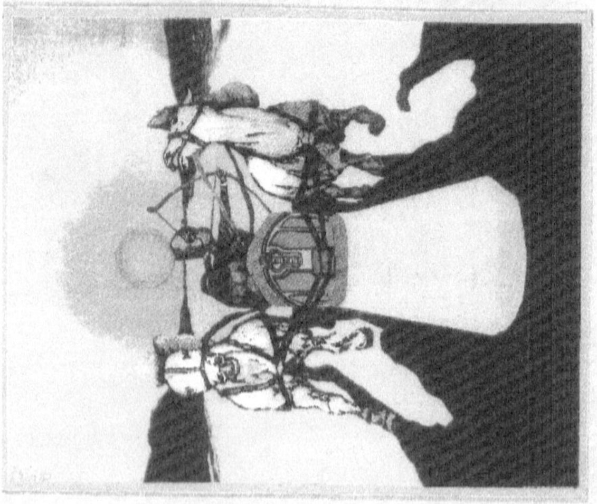

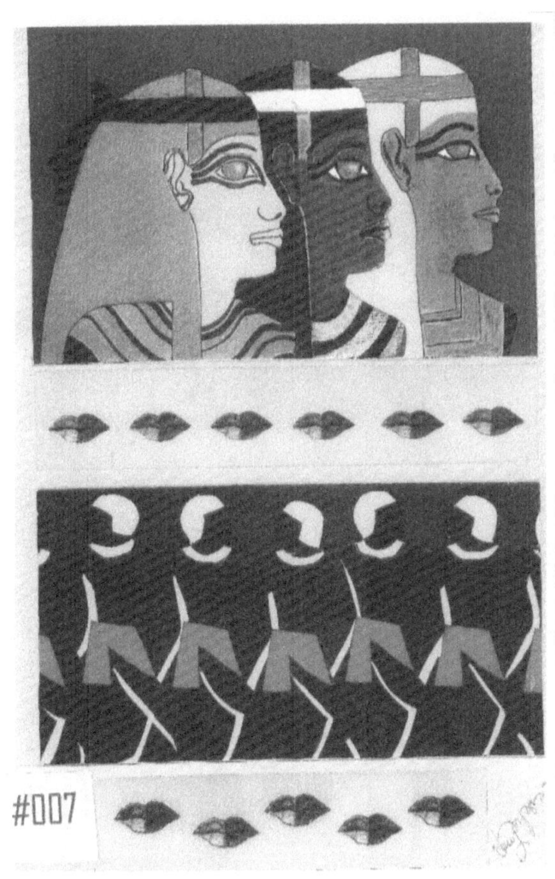

#007

PHARAOH'S
MOUNTAIN
Nuba
Covered Lower Valley
of River Nile...
ABOUT
EGYPT
BEN EL SHARNA
OASIS
ROUTE
THEBES
NORTH
...And there nursed the doubtful
child of civilization
MASSEUSES'
FROM "THE RECLUSE OF MIN"
PROFICIENT IN USE OF ALCOHOL,
ABORATIONS AND HARMONIES.
"The Nubian Pharaoh"
#008

Nuba!
Covered Lower Valley
of River Nile...
ANCIENT EGYPT
TEL-EL-AMARNA
OASIS FAYUM
THEBES
NORTH
...And there nursed the doubtful
child of civilization
PHARAOH'S
MOUNTAIN
MASSEUSES'
FROM "THE RECLUSE OF MIR"
PROFICIENT IN USE OF ALCOHOL,
ADORATIONS AND HARMONIES.
"The Naked Pharaoh"
#009

#011

#013

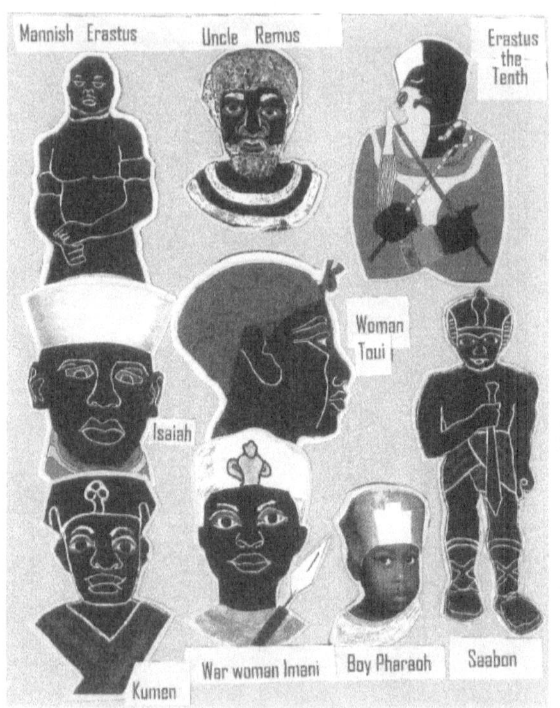

Mannish Erastus
Uncle Remus
Erastus the Tenth
Woman Toui
Isaiah
Kumen
War woman Imani
Boy Pharaoh
Saabon
#014

www.ingramcontent.com/pod-product-compliance
Lightning Source LLC
Chambersburg PA
CBHW031338060726
47590CB00007B/2532